W9-BSH-340

The Shoemaker's Gospel

the
shoemaker's
gospel
a novel

DANIEL BRENT

LOYOLAPRESS.

CHICAGO

LOYOLAPRESS.
3441 N. ASHLAND AVENUE
CHICAGO, ILLINOIS 60657
(800) 621-1008
WWW.LOYOLABOOKS.ORG

*Cover photo by Todd Gipstein/CORBIS. Additional cover
photography by Phil Martin.*

*Cover design by Rick Franklin
Interior design by Kathryn Seckman Kirsch*

Library of Congress Cataloging-in-Publication Data
Brent, Daniel.
  The shoemaker's Gospel : a novel / Daniel Brent.
    p. cm.
  ISBN-13: 978-0-8294-2394-5
  ISBN-10: 0-8294-2394-X
  I. Title.
PS3602.R456S56 2006
813'.6—dc22

                              2006009927

Printed in the United States of America
06 07 08 09 10 Bang 10 9 8 7 6 5 4 3 2 1

To Betsy, Megan, and Maura,
the three women in my life who have modeled
for me the ideals and sensitivity of Jesus.

Table *of* Contents

Author's Preface

Few scholars of the Christian Scriptures believe that the Gospels were written by the apostles Matthew and John and two hangers-on, Mark and Luke. Although the written documents appeared decades after the death of Jesus, they represented an effort to preserve in writing the deeds and sayings of the Teacher.

Mainstream Christian scholars agree that the literary style used by the Gospel authors allowed them great latitude in how they put together their own accounts of Jesus, using the stories recalled and passed along by the Christian communities of the first century. Through the centuries, we Christians have continued to recapture Jesus and plumb the significance of his message for our lives and times. The Church believes that, through the Spirit of God, we can continue to discover what Jesus' life and message mean to us, in every age.

My daughter once challenged me to identify four people—past or present, real or fictitious—

whom I would want to meet over lunch. I chose Jesus, Paul, Ben Franklin, and my father, who had died when I was young. One day I thought it might be interesting to create those luncheon conversations from my imagination, helped by what I knew about the personalities. My fascination with the lunchtime discussion that I might have had with Jesus led to the initial notes that eventually became this book.

The model for meditation given us by St. Ignatius of Loyola suggests that we re-create in our imagination the scenes of Gospel accounts and then place ourselves in these scenes. We watch and we listen. And in that context, we meet the Spirit of Jesus directing us still. We are not merely exercising our imagination but making a pilgrimage.

This book is the result of such meditation. The events, though plausible and often based on the Gospel stories, have issued from my imagination. In faith I can say that those imaginings developed in the context of prayer and so were to some extent led by the Spirit of Jesus. The character and message of Jesus as you will find them here reflect the Jesus I have grown to know since my childhood—a person specific to my memories and experiences. In putting this account together, I undertook to reread the Scripture accounts with my heart and my intuition. As in the meditation format of St. Ignatius, I listened to the locusts and the crickets as well as to the man. I let my imagination fill in scenes and conversations. I've tried to feel the emotion in the stories Jesus told and the conversations he had. I put myself into the character of the shoemaker and listened to the Teacher. I walked with the disciples and listened to their conversations, watched their expressions and their actions.

My hope is that you will enter the story as well. Perhaps these stories of mine will lead you to your own and enhance your ongoing pilgrimage of the Spirit.

A Word from the Shoemaker

I'm an old man now.

And an old man is entitled to savor his memories and reflections. I look back on my life and am astonished at what it's given me. I live now in hope of what is yet in store in a life to come, when I will once again see the Teacher.

This story began when I was barely more than a boy. My father was Isaac, a shoemaker in Capernaum, well liked and fairly prosperous for a tradesman, at least by standards of the time. He was a widower, my mother having died before I was old enough to remember her. He had promised her that I would be educated, and he was conscientious, almost obsessive, about that promise. He sent me to the small temple school every morning. In the afternoons and on school holidays he taught me his trade. There was no work on the Sabbath, of course, but we would go to the synagogue and then he would read to me from scrolls he'd borrowed from anywhere he could, mostly from the scribes themselves.

I always saw my father as old. I realize now that he was actually quite young. One day I came home from school to find that he had died suddenly at his workbench. He was all I had, and his death devastated me. But I had no time to wallow in grief. With the help and encouragement—insistence, rather—of the scribes Isaac had befriended, I took over his shoemaking business. What I didn't yet know about making shoes, I learned quickly from necessity. As it turned out, my father had been a very good teacher.

So if my business didn't flourish at first, at least it provided for my needs and gave me enough leisure to continue some informal studies and reading. I loved the Scriptures. That was fortunate because little else was available for me to read. I would often go to the synagogue to read scrolls that I wasn't, of course, allowed to take home. What reading materials I could find, plus the modest collection that my father had acquired, I read over and over.

As I was able to afford it, I began to purchase writing materials from the caravans that regularly traveled through Capernaum right past my shop. I developed some skill in writing, awkwardly at first. Often, at the end of the day I would write down my thoughts by the light of the old oil lamp that my father had treasured. Writing words on a page helped me understand my own thinking about life and God and politics and relationships. And perhaps because it allowed me to express the emotions I would not show outwardly, it helped me to come to terms with the cruelty of my being left an orphan too soon.

Two years after my father's death, the Teacher passed through my life.

I had settled into a routine. I was comfortable with my trade by then, and my business was doing reasonably well. Many of my friends had married. Some had moved away. Occasionally I would make a trip to Jerusalem with some neighbors for one of the feasts. Those trips afforded me the opportunity to enjoy the welcome of former schoolmates who now lived there. I'd also discovered that, in Jerusalem, I could purchase some exotic leathers that I'd not seen in Capernaum except on the feet of highly placed Roman officials.

I had first laid eyes on the Teacher at the Jordan during my second trip to Jerusalem. I was astonished some weeks later to discover that he was in Capernaum, speaking to the small groups that found him at the shore of our lake. I began to use what little bit of free time I had to go down to the lake—it was only a ten-minute walk—to listen to him. Often in the evening, I'd write out notes to recapture what he'd said or done that day.

It has been more than forty years since those heady days when Jesus taught at the lake and so many of us had the extraordinary opportunity to listen to him. Not long after his death, I married. My wife bore us five children, and three of them are still alive, though for these past ten years I have been alone again. I now have my first grandchild, a little girl named Martha whom I love dearly.

I still have the shop at the same location in Capernaum, though now I work less and read more and take long walks to the places where Jesus taught. I can still see the crowds and hear his voice. I sometimes fantasize that I hear him call me. "Hello, Soft Shoes. Come sit with me." Then I feel as if part of my soul has been stolen away, and I long to be with him.

These years have revealed to me what a privilege it was to have known him and to have witnessed all that happened during those days. Often I regret that I left Jerusalem the day after his death. Otherwise, I almost certainly would have been with one of the groups that he appeared to during the weeks that followed.

But then, after a time, when it became clear that his return to us was not going to happen the next day nor the day after that, life settled down. His followers went less and less often to the synagogues—and, frankly, were less and less welcome there. Those of us who had followed him met on the first day of the week instead of on the Sabbath. We discovered that there were many more of us than I would have guessed, even having seen the crowds in Galilee on their best days. We gathered wherever there was a welcoming space; we shared the stories about him; and we broke his bread and drank his cup.

Most of those who traveled and ministered with him have, over the years, assumed roles of leadership. They have the best stories, and they also have credibility that others do not. Many of them have gone abroad, convinced that it was Jesus' expectation that they take his message to the Gentiles. And a zealous new witness, Paul from Tarsus, has joined Jesus' disciples to preach his message in Corinth and even Rome. Some of those in Jesus' inner circle have died or been killed. Jesus' relatives are represented mostly by James, who, after the crucifixion of Jesus, came to accept him as God's messenger. James has become Jesus' chief witness in Judea even though he did not actually hear or see most of Jesus' activity.

I have noticed that, as the original witnesses have gotten older, the stories have become more condensed. Many of the details have dropped out, and sometimes the stories have been recast so that those who were there would barely recognize them. At first I was distressed by this development. But then I decided that Jesus himself would not be unhappy with it. The soul of his message remains intact. And, in fact, if the stories are easier to remember and their points less likely to be missed, he would be happy with that outcome. Besides, he promised an Advocate who would stay with us when he was gone. The evolution of the stories is, I think, one of the ways in which we feel that presence.

So this little band that gathered regularly on the shores of the Sea of Galilee to learn from the master has grown and embraced many times the number of people his voice reached when he was here among us. And his story is rapidly becoming an epic song that uses the same sequence and the same stanzas whenever and wherever it is sung.

And whenever we gather to sing that tale and break his bread, I can feel him here still. He is telling us about the steadfastness of his Father's love. He is challenging us to attend to the widow and the poor and the orphan and the sick. He is reminding us of a kingdom that we are destined to inherit as his brothers and sisters. And he is embracing us still with those deep eyes and that resonant voice.

I have been so singularly blessed to be one of the participants in that great drama that God staged to recast history. More than Adam, Noah, Abraham, Moses, or David, it is in Jesus that God has redesigned his relationship with his people. And I was there! I wish now that I could give even one day of my experiences at that lake to my granddaughter, Martha. But it cannot be. And so here, years after I wrote them, I prepare to pass these feeble notes on to her: a legacy from a grandfather. I wish that I had captured more of the dialogue, more of the detail, more of the stories and events.

But it is what it is, this account. I hope that, as little Martha comes to know this Jesus in the community of his followers who are her contemporaries, she will find in these pages a glimpse of this lord and teacher and friend of her grandfather, Soft Shoes.

The River

1

Jesus' Baptism

The human condition weeps for redemption, and I will speak to it with acts, not just words.

At the Jordan today I saw a charismatic figure whose name, I'm told, is Jesus. My home and business are in Capernaum, but I've been in Jerusalem for a week doing some business and visiting friends. Around Jerusalem I'd heard stories of John the baptizer. Friends who have gone out to the river to see him have returned with stories about his preaching. His message is a scolding one: None of us are living as

God expects, and it is time to straighten out our lives, or else.

The "or else" part isn't clear but we know it isn't good—God's hammer is raised! On days when the religious leaders appear at the river, John is especially fascinating. He shifts his attention to them and scolds with great fury. For some mysterious reason the leaders go out to hear John more often than you would think they'd *want* to go. My guess is that some went at first just to see for themselves what John was doing and saying. The political situation in Palestine is touchy. The religious leaders have learned how to protect some of our freedoms under Roman rule. Their side of the bargain requires that they neither make nor allow political waves. So if something—or someone—might be making trouble, it needs to be investigated. At least it bears watching.

I suspect that the first religious leaders to venture to John's performance at the Jordan expected to stand unnoticed at the edge of the crowd. Unhappily for them, I'm told, the crowds were not as large as the stories had led them to believe, and there was really nowhere to hide. They weren't savvy enough to go in disguise. Obviously they did not expect to draw John's special attention. They probably expected to discredit him by contrasting his simple message with their thorough understanding of the Law.

In any case, he did notice them, and now each time they come, he singles them out with his finger-pointing tirades. He's been telling them that they're scoundrels, much to the delight of many in his audience. John's words undoubtedly have the ring of truth when he calls these leaders hypocrites who put burdens on others that they would not carry themselves. Some of us have felt their judgment, spoken or otherwise. Yet John says that, far from setting the standard and being worthy to judge the holiness of others, they are the worst of sinners, made so because they stand on God's shoulders to show off how righteous they are.

On days when the religious leaders do not appear—and, not surprisingly, they aren't appearing so often now—the Baptizer turns his wrath on ordinary folk, accusing them of being cheats, liars, adulterers—whatever—and threatening them with hellfire. God's wrath can be escaped, he tells them, only by a radical conversion in their lives, a turning back to the Lord and a renouncing of their evil ways. As evidence of their change of heart they are welcome to wade into the river and have him baptize them, symbolically washing away the grime of their sinfulness.

I have gone out to the river on two of the days I've been in Jerusalem. On the first occasion I listened spellbound and went down to the river to be baptized myself. It seemed impossible not to get caught up in the enthusiasm of the moment and the man. My second time at the river was today, and I just stood at the edge of the crowd and listened.

That's when Jesus showed up. John hadn't noticed him, or didn't recognize him, until Jesus stepped into the river to be baptized. John recoiled. He looked flustered, and suddenly he was speechless. It was such a complete change of mood that everyone in the crowd knew instantly that something was happening.

John said something to Jesus to the effect that his baptizing of him would be inappropriate. "You baptize me instead," is what I remember hearing. Jesus, however, insisted on being baptized by John. "The human condition weeps for redemption, and I will speak to it with acts, not just words," he said. John complied, but did not look at ease as he did so. What happened then I'm not sure. Others standing near me said they heard a loud voice from somewhere. I thought I heard a clap of thunder, but as I remember, there wasn't even a cloud in the sky. A stunned silence followed. I don't know how Jesus left, and I learned only later who he was. After baptizing this Jesus, John stood motionless in the river, silent and shaken, while people slipped away. He was still there when I left.

The Lake

Importance of Example

Be careful not to gloat over the praise your good deeds bring.

My home is on the main street that runs through Capernaum. I live simply, with a kitchen area just large enough to hold a table where I usually eat. I also have a small bedroom. Since my father's death, I've taken out his bed and built a small writing desk and shelving to hold my scrolls and writing materials. The main front room now houses the shoemaker's workbench that my father had squeezed into the bedroom area. I enjoy being able to see out the front window while

I work. This arrangement also allows me to present an attractive reception area for customers. I have there a round table and four handsome straight chairs along with two comfortable green fabric chairs my father acquired years ago.

Today at the shore of Capernaum's sea, Jesus talked to a small crowd. He talked about words and behavior. I've been going to the lake frequently now to hear him. He is captivating as a speaker, and his message somehow rings goodness to my soul.

It was surprising to discover that the figure I had seen at the river in Judea had now appeared in our community and was preaching on the shores of our quiet lake. Nothing ever happens in Capernaum. The sun rises; the sun sets. The late mornings bring the smell of the sea as the fishermen bring their catches in and move them to market. Old Philip, who keeps a garden in a small plot of land behind my shop, pushes the hoe through his plantings, tilling his hopes and giving some exercise to his two dogs, who chase and bark at him if nothing else is moving. A highlight of life here is the occasional caravan coming up the road headed for the fork to Damascus or to Zenoff's inn at the top of the hill. The caravans themselves would likely be dull were it not for the chasing and shouting of the children who always run alongside to tease the animals and beg for treats or coins from the caravan masters.

So anything out of the ordinary gets noticed. Weddings, funerals, and births become everyone's business. For me, even finishing or selling a pair of shoes is a special event.

So the appearance of this preacher in our community has raised a great deal of interest. It would be an exaggeration to say that everyone goes to hear him, but some days it seems that the whole town is there. His message seems to be broader and more complex than that of John at the Jordan. And while he is not reluctant to scold and threaten, his message strikes me as more balanced. And he is approachable, even likeable. The children are comfortable with him, and I leave the sessions at the lake feeling refreshed. He assures us that, even on our most difficult days, we live in the embrace of a loving Father.

At the same time, his words do not set a soul completely at ease. Often he makes me feel that there is much about myself that either I don't know or don't want to examine too closely. I don't consider myself a great sinner, but on the days I listen to him, I leave more aware of the gaps between the behavior he calls for and the realities of my life. Today was an example.

His message went something like this. "If you say to others, 'Do this,' and you don't do it yourself, then your words are empty. You must behave in a way consistent with your words or you are just a hypocrite. You can tell your children, for example, what you expect of them, but if they don't see you behaving in that way, then your words are wasted. You are a bell without a clapper. If they can't see the wisdom of your words acted out in your own life, then even your children will dismiss your words as meaningless. Besides, it is the example that gives clarity to the words. You cannot teach a skill by saying 'Do this; do that.' You must show someone how to do it as well as talk about it. They will learn more with their eyes than they can learn with their ears."

At this point, a sly smile came to his face. "But beware of this," he said. "If your motive is just to show off, then your otherwise good example can be corrupted. If I behave in such and such a way so that others will think well of me and say, 'Look how good or clever or generous or pious he is,' then the merit of what would have been my good example is destroyed by my motive. This is my quarrel with our religious leaders. Some of their practices are superficial. But if they did them out of pure motives, misled though the behaviors may be, I would not be so distressed with them as I am when I see them performing for public praise.

"So the good examples we set must be motivated by our genuine conviction that these are the right things to do. Do not hide your good works. It is good that others see them, learn from them, and are motivated by them to do similar good works. We learn virtue from virtuous people. But be careful not to gloat over the praise your good deeds bring or the reputation they build for you. Goodness is not about how you are seen but about who you are!"

I returned to the shop this afternoon expecting to repair some sandals that I'd promised would be ready tomorrow. I sat at my workbench and took my tools from their cabinet. But my mind was so occupied with what I had heard and with the character of this teacher that I could not make my head and my hands work together. I finally gave up and went out to sit in the shade of the overhang and to sift through the thoughts and questions cascading through my mind.

It has been many generations since a prophet was seen and heard in Israel. Is it possible that I am a witness to the next prophet? That's unlikely. Yet the man speaks with such conviction and his message does have the sound of a challenge coming directly from the Lord. At least it sounds that way to this little shoemaker in this little town. But isn't that exactly what makes it so unlikely?

Soft Shoes

The workbench is as much God's place as the temple.

I saw him briefly this morning. I'd gone out of the shop for some fresh air when he came by with a few of his intimates. They were laughing. The one named Thomas—Jesus calls him South Wind—was telling a story about one of his customers who had tried to cheat him, got caught, and then made up an outrageous story to explain that it had been an honest mistake. They were headed for the lake, and Jesus was in a jovial mood. I think he enjoys Thomas, who has a clever sense of humor.

Surely that must be a great tonic for a preacher whose message is not always popular or happily received.

I could not join them. But I stood at the door of my shop and watched as they passed. Jesus recognized me and called over, "Good morning, Soft Shoes." He has a nickname for everybody. He must have seen the disappointment on my face. He held my eyes for a moment and added, "The workbench is as much God's place as the temple."

Jesus lives not far from me on the west edge of town, about a ten-minute walk away. He stays in a modest outer apartment at Zenoff's inn. The traders on the small caravans headed both east and west stop there to eat, spend the night, and rest their animals. I go there myself occasionally for a meal or a social evening. Zenoff's wife is a commendable cook, and Zenoff makes a congenial bartender and host. I think he trades Jesus lodging in return for some carpentry services and small chores around the place. In addition to the main inn and the apartment, Zenoff has a shelter for the animals, and he keeps two or three donkeys of his own. He sometimes rides one himself but mostly, I think, he makes a little profit by buying and selling or bartering them with the caravan chiefs. He will pick up an animal that's sick, nurse it to health, and have it ready to sell to a later caravan. One mirthful night at the inn, I heard Zenoff tell the story of how he sold a donkey back to its original owner on his return trip. He'd made a handsome gain by simply giving the animal a few weeks' rest.

I'm not certain but I think that, when the inn is very crowded, Jesus moves out of the apartment so Zenoff can rent it. I think Jesus then stays with admirers in town or sometimes goes out into the desert to spend the night. He is a prayerful, reflective man, and I'm sure that there are times, even when the inn is not crowded, that the noise of reveling there would not be conducive to prayer or reflection or even sleep! The few times I've been there I've never seen him join the reveling. Once I saw him take supper there. He was with a couple of his intimates, and they appeared to enjoy themselves but were gone before the serious drinking started.

❧ 4 ❧

The Exorcism

I was there this morning to reclaim the woman from Satan.

Apparently Jesus had a difficult day today. I wasn't there this morning, but the regulars told me he went through a kind of ritual in which he behaved quite strangely. It happened in front of the inn. He was confronting a woman, shouting and snarling in her face, barking at her in what the observers said was gibberish. Some said he was drooling as though he were having a fit, but others said no, that his shouting was creating spit.

All in all, they said, it was an ugly sight to witness, and it lasted perhaps five minutes.

It seems that some family or friends of the woman thought she was possessed by a devil, and they perceived Jesus as a holy man and wanted him to cure her. Probably wanting to avoid the crowd at the lake, they brought her to Zenoff's and found him there as he was leaving. Already at the inn were a few of the regulars who often walk with him to the lake and, of course, the guests at the inn who heard the commotion and came out. The woman and Jesus began to shout at each other in that strange language. People said they were ready to intervene if the confrontation came to blows. By the time it was over, some of the men had come from the synagogue. I don't know whether they had heard the argument or someone went to alert them.

Eventually the woman calmed down and began to speak normally. My friends reported that she could not remember any of the incident. The people who had brought her were elated. Jesus too had calmed down, and he received their profuse thanks, making little or no comment to them. The group left, taking the woman with them and explaining to her all that had happened. Jesus' followers said that he was exhausted and quiet after the woman and her family left. He did not go down to the lake.

I heard the reports at my shop in the early afternoon and went over to the inn. I thought I would be casual and just see what was happening. Sure enough, Jesus was there talking with a small group. It did not seem that I was out of place so I sat down in the back circle and listened. "The people from the synagogue were not impressed," one of his friends reported to him. "I heard two of them saying that you used Satan's power to drive out that devil from her."

"If they thought about it," Jesus said, "they would know that Satan driving out Satan makes no sense. If Satan's kingdom is having a civil war, then he will destroy himself without our having to deal with him. But that isn't the case. We must confront and fight Satan where and when we find him.

"Isn't it interesting that when I drive out devils they say it is Satan's accomplishment. That's because they don't like or trust me. I don't think they disagree with the lessons I teach, but they don't appreciate that I criticize the demands they make upon the people. My criticism of their rules makes them nervous. They are afraid that I am chipping the mortar out from between the bricks of the edifice they've built. It's a temple of man-made bricks that confines people, that makes them feel guilty and repentant about the wrong things. Does God really care how often we wash our hands? But God cares about the widow, and they would have us ignore her or, at most, see her as a social problem."

Zenoff's wife came around to bring some biscuits and to take drink orders. Jesus thanked her and waited while she took care of her tasks. Then he continued.

"They see me as undermining their authority and so they feel obliged to look for reasons to fault everything I say or do. But think about it. When their people drive out devils, by whose power is it done? By Satan's or by God's? If they think devils are driven out by Satan's power, then they condemn their own people. But if devils are driven out by God's power, then clearly the power of God was present this morning."

He was speaking quietly, thoughtfully. He still looked and sounded very weary. I'd heard stories of earlier confrontations he'd had with possessed people but none as detailed as those I'd heard about today's encounter. What I'd gathered was that they were always raucous engagements and that Jesus' behavior in those incidents seemed out of character, even crazy.

"The incident this morning looked almost like a street fight," Simon said to Jesus. Simon is one of the fishermen. I've noticed him close to Jesus in the crowd each time I've been to the lake. "We didn't know what to do, with the two of you screaming at each other like that. We thought it was going to come to punches."

"I've not found an easy way to do battle with the devil," Jesus replied. "I was there this morning to reclaim the woman from Satan. You don't just walk into Satan's house and walk out with what you want. You either strike a bargain or you incapacitate Satan so that you can take what you came for. I was in a fight with Satan, not the woman. I won, and I reclaimed the woman for her family."

"Jesus," commented Thomas, "you just compared yourself to a robber! The men up the street in the synagogue would love that!"

The remark broke the tension, and no one laughed harder than Jesus. He suddenly looked relaxed and energetic again. "It is always warmer when the South Wind blows," Jesus teased Thomas. Shortly after this conversation, the group broke up and Jesus went back to his apartment. There was to be no afternoon trip to the lake on this day.

❦ 5 ❧

Family Conflict

*We follow the light we have and fulfill our
duties as we see them.*

Today a small group of his relatives showed up at the inn. Word of the incident yesterday with the possessed woman had reached Nazareth. Most of his relatives, the men especially, were willing to dismiss it. I suppose that when someone like Jesus grows up into a life of itinerant preaching, those who have grown up around him understand that he's not quite like most people. His relatives seem to have found Jesus likeable enough and very bright and very "religious." What bothered them was that he chose not to use the "normal" vocations available. Why didn't he just study to be a rabbi or a Pharisee? Why must he wander from town to town and draw attention to himself? If he didn't like joining the established religious world, he could just marry and settle down and be a carpenter. His father, Joseph, had taught him the trade, and he was more than competent at it.

His mother was worried about him. Earlier stories had come back that his behavior in Capernaum sometimes bordered on crazy, and she thought perhaps he should come home for a while. At her insistence, the men came with her to Capernaum to check on Jesus. They talked with Zenoff and a few others who had witnessed the encounter with the possessed woman. John (Jesus calls him Thunder Two; his brother James is Thunder One) and I had come early to the apartment to help Jesus repair a problem with the back wall. As we worked, John and I overheard one awkward conversation. One of Jesus' relatives scolded him for his lifestyle.

"You have no regular income or livelihood. Your friends at least work so they can afford the luxury of sitting around for half the day listening to you. But you preach only when you please. From what I hear there are days, sometimes days on end, when you do nothing. If I did nothing for days on end, people would call me irresponsible—and rightly so!"

Jesus responded to him, "We follow the light we have and fulfill our duties as we see them. And within our different callings are seasons. The birds don't build their nests every month but only when there will be young who have need of them. Even the grapevines rest. If we worry them into producing out of season, this does a disservice to them and to the vineyard keeper."

He didn't sound impatient but was simply trying to reason with his relatives. I wondered if the message might be intended more for those of us, such as John and me, who were within hearing.

Jesus idly ran his hand over some of the repair work that John and I had been doing. Force of habit, I suspect, for a man trained as a carpenter. I felt awkward, not sure of how a professional would assess our crude work. But he didn't comment on it. Instead he continued his explanation, this time turning to his mother.

"Listen. I'd like you and everyone to stop in at the dining room and have something to eat before you make the trip back. Tell Zenoff and his wife to put the cost on my bill," he said with a twinkle in his voice. Then he looked at me. "This is Soft Shoes, a friend of mine," he said. And then to me, "Would you show them to the dining room and make sure they are taken care of?"

I led them into the courtyard and back to the dining room. Zenoff himself welcomed us and saw that everyone was comfortable. I was bold enough to join them—there were seven in the group—and sat down next to his mother. Her name is Mary.

It was not yet noon, and the room was empty except for us. Zenoff and his wife were delighted to see the group. They served tea and wine and set to preparing food.

I was brimming with questions about Jesus, and Mary was very friendly and talkative. Yes, she told me, Jesus had learned the carpentry trade from his father, Joseph, who had died a few years ago. From his early years he'd seen himself as called to be a messenger for his heavenly Father, and while he loved Joseph a great deal, he'd always known that the time would come when he would have to leave Nazareth. It was heartbreaking when he left home, but, she confessed, she knew that he was destined for that. She had dedicated her own life to God's service, and there was no way her own preferences would get in the way of God's plans for her son.

"How do you manage without him?" I asked her.

"He and my husband left some savings," she explained, "and everyone takes care to see that I have what I need."

"Everyone?" I wondered aloud.

"Everyone in Nazareth knows everyone else," she explained. "And half of them, I think, are related to us. Benjamin—he's the stocky one at the other table—stops in almost every day to be sure I'm managing. I rarely need help but he appreciates how lonely it is for me, and he'll sit and chat and bring me up to date on the town's news. He usually hears the stories of what Jesus is doing before I do."

The heavyset man to whom she referred was the one who had just accused Jesus of being irresponsible. "Earlier it sounded like Benjamin is unhappy with Jesus," I said.

"Benjamin worries about Jesus but, of course, Benjamin worries about everything." She gave a little smile. "He knows there is something special about Jesus. He can't understand how God sometimes leads us in strange ways. He'd like everyone to do what he himself would do. After hearing about what happened here yesterday, it was Benjamin who thought we should come and talk with Jesus."

"Well, this morning he didn't seem to bend the course that Jesus is on, did he?" I ventured.

"No." She arched an eyebrow knowingly. "Jesus knows what his father wants, and he'll let nothing get in the way of that. I was not surprised by his reaction. I'm sad that we've upset him like this. But I thought it was a good idea to invite him to come home for a while."

I thought it interesting that she talked about his father as God rather than her husband.

"You should stay for a day or two and listen to him talk to us down at the lake," I said. "The lessons he teaches are challenging and wise. It is the very voice of God that we hear there."

"You are more correct on that than you realize," she said. "He has been consumed with God's message since he was a little boy. And you must remember that I had him to myself for several years before he began this itinerant preaching."

Her face had taken on a look of sadness. The beautiful brown eyes were showing lines of worry. She looked down at the table.

"You're concerned about him," I said. Proclaimer of the obvious; it's a talent of mine!

"John, the one they know as the Baptist, is my nephew. I knew him before he was born. And now he has been arrested and jailed because they don't want to hear his message. They don't want to hear what God demands of them. And now I fear for John's life."

"You fear that Jesus will suffer a similar fate," I said.

"And for the same reason."

At this point Zenoff's wife appeared with platters of fish smothered in a lemon sauce, side dishes of turnips, and baskets of bread with oil. "It is an honor to serve the family of Jesus," she announced. "And you cannot leave for your journey home with empty stomachs."

If the failure of their mission had dulled their appetites, the aroma of the food corrected that and everyone ate heartily. Toward the end of the meal, Jesus came in and sat with us next to his mother. He asked about the health of one of his uncles who had been ill, and they talked about goings-on at Nazareth. When the group rose to leave, Jesus and his mother embraced and Jesus expressed appreciation to each of the men who had made the trip to accompany her. By the time they'd all thanked Zenoff and his wife for the hospitality, the dining room was beginning to fill with people coming for lunch. I saw Mary out to the street. Zenoff's wife followed us out, and I left the two women to their conversation. When I returned to the dining room, Jesus was gone.

Meekness

How many times has God chosen the weak
to baffle the strong?

Jesus showed up this morning at the lake with his beard neatly trimmed. I think Zenoff's wife persuaded him that he would look less intimidating that way. She probably trimmed it herself. I wouldn't be surprised if Jesus' mother, Mary put her up to it. When they get together, women have conspiratorial ways that even God will not intrude upon.

As we waited for Jesus to start, John awkwardly complimented him on how coolheaded and understanding he had been yesterday with his family. "It would have been easy to get provoked into an argument with the one who called you irresponsible," John said.

"That was Benjamin," Jesus responded. "I love him. He's the one who looks after my mother and makes sure she has what she needs. What I especially admire about him, though, is his detachment. He is careful and sensible about his money. But he's not at all attached to it or to anything it can buy. He has no need of the luxuries he could afford. And he's generous. If someone has an honest need, Benjamin is always there for him.

"If only everyone were as unattached to their worldly goods as Benjamin is. Really, this quality is unrelated to how much money a person has. For one person, gathering wealth is a preoccupation. Another looks just to what's needed for the day and trusts that God—and an honest day's work—will provide for tomorrow.

"So a poor man can be just as greedy as a rich man. And a rich man can be just as detached, as poor in spirit, as a poor man. The quality relates to wealth of character."

John raised another question. "Does it bother you that your closest relatives have not become followers of your preaching?"

Jesus did not answer right away. Then his words were careful. "It hurts. You want your family to understand who you are and what you are called to do. And I am disappointed for them—they don't come and listen to my message."

John continued, "Haven't they seen the wonders you do?"

Of course I'd heard the stories of Jesus curing people at the lake, but I had never been there to witness any of it. I'm hesitant to disbelieve those accounts but I'm also skeptical.

"No," he answered. "I will not show off for them. And there has not been an occasion in Nazareth for me to do anything special when I've had the opportunity to deliver my message there. They've heard the stories of my works, and, of course, they can't explain them. But neither will they draw any conclusions from them. In fact I think sometimes they resent being asked to explain how it's possible that I can say and do what's attributed to me."

"So they just pretend that it's not happening," said John.

"It seems so. Perhaps they consider the questions to be an attack on them personally. Maybe the implication is, 'How could peasants like you, with little or no education, produce this?' I can understand if they're embarrassed by such remarks."

"The one named James seems to hang back from criticizing you," John ventured.

"Yes, I think James may be the exception," Jesus said. "I think that, because he knows my background and education, he considers it miraculous that I can do any of this. I think he sees the power of God in that. But I believe he's reluctant to argue with the others."

"It's like the brothers of Joseph or David. They were too close to the situation to see it clearly," John mused.

"You're probably right. You judge me based on what you hear and see. They judge me based on my origins. The Baptizer is a cousin of ours, and he also has misgivings about me and my mission. A prophet must stand alone and apart. It has always been that way. There is no chorus to join and support him in the confrontations of his calling."

When the crowd had settled down, Jesus talked to us about meekness. "When Jonah felt weak and inadequate to the task God had given him, his preaching was effective. Within days the great city of Nineveh was reduced to conversion and penance. But Jonah had become impressed with what he was accomplishing and began to savor the impending destruction of the city, which he had predicted. When God was moved to compassion and spared the city, Jonah sniveled and pouted. How many times has God chosen the weak to baffle the strong? And how many times have the powerful been reduced to ashes because they felt invulnerable?"

He paused and looked across the crowd, then smiled and gestured broadly with his arms. "This is not *my* personal message! How many times has God taught his people that the meek are blessed and will inherit his favor! If you are not worried about tomorrow because you feel safe in the care of a loving Father, then your peace of mind is blessed. If you are not worried about tomorrow because you have stores of plenty, then beware. For God has the option of stripping those all away!"

Reaction to John's Murder

God's plan will not be thwarted.

This morning word came to the lake that Herod had executed John the baptizer. Jesus was greatly upset. And saddened. But he said nothing to the crowd about it. He did tell this story.

"A king put on a great banquet and was caught up completely in the revelry. As the evening grew late, one of his soldiers rushed into the hall to see him. 'Our enemy is approaching the palace and we are in great danger,' he reported. 'This is no time for news like that,' shouted the king, who was more than a little inebriated. 'See how upset you are making my guests? Besides, look at you! You have barged into my party without even being dressed for an occasion like this.'

"With that the king ordered that the soldier be arrested, taken away, and executed. Then the king returned to his party. Within the hour, the enemy's troops breached the palace's unprepared defenses, killed the king, and took the revelers into slavery.

"If you can hear, pay attention to the lesson. The time grows late, and the opportunity to prepare will soon be spent."

Jesus spoke only briefly on this day and then asked Simon and a few of his other intimates to take him out in the boat away from the crowd. I later asked Andrew, Simon's brother and a customer of mine, what happened.

Andrew is taller than his brother Simon. He has the same dark eyes, and while his height gives him the appearance of being thin, he is strong. The work of managing their boat and hauling nets has given him muscles that contradict the soft appearance of his face. He tends to be quiet, often deferring to his older, stockier brother. And sometimes there is a squinting look on his face that betrays his struggle to understand what Jesus' teachings may require from him. I think Andrew is one of those people who is always searching for more in life—to understand what things mean and what he must do. It appears that he is finding some answers to those questions as he listens to Jesus.

"When we went out in the boat, Jesus was silent for a long time," Andrew told me. "He looked so sad—and his eyes were wet. He was slumped over like someone who was frustrated or defeated. After we had been out for an hour or more, he began to talk, but in a soft voice, almost to himself.

"He didn't mention Herod by name. But the anger came through his voice when he condemned those who use power to take from the weak their dignity and property and sometimes even their lives. For people to do those things, Jesus said, is to rain God's anger on themselves. God is, after all, the source of all power, he said, and to use power to protect power, or to promote one's own pitiful ends, is to spit in the face of the Lord.

"He was quiet again, for a long time," Andrew continued. "He just kept shaking his head slowly, in disbelief. Finally he began to speak about John. He admired John's complete dedication to the mission God had given him. 'Not the greatest prophets, not Isaiah, Elijah, not Ezekiel, not even, I think, Abraham or Moses were more invested in their mission to Israel than this simple man who stood at the Jordan and alerted us that God's time had come. His fasting, his prayer, his daring preaching invited many, a great many, to the conversion of heart that God requires.'

"Then Jesus said, 'Most of you would probably not be with me if it were not for John. And many of those at the lake today are with us because John turned their hearts and then pointed them to me.' He shook his head then and said, 'God's plan will not be thwarted. But woe to him who snatched John away from the wilderness and silenced the voice that spoke for God!'"

By now, I could see how sad Andrew was, too. Now that the shock has worn off about the news of John's death, I feel the loss acutely. It was John who moved me and who introduced me to Jesus. I am one of those people Jesus spoke of.

8

Peacemakers

Does God not have the right to ask you first
to set aside not just your weapon but also
the anger that led you to pick it up?

B lessed are those who make peace; they are
the children of the Lord.

This was the gist of his message today.
It was a message that fit the day. The weather was
cool and clear. A soft breeze off the lake made it
more comfortable to sit and listen. He told us that
God's preference would be for us to live out our
days in peace with time to make our contribution
to the world, raise our children, and spend our

energy doing our work and appreciating the presence of the Creator in the good things about us.

"But pride and selfishness lead to conflict and war. Those who instigate or promote wars will be held responsible for the widows and orphans that they create. God calls you to be peacemakers. You've heard it said, 'An eye for an eye and a tooth for a tooth.' But you who are my followers are not to behave that way. When you strike back at the man who would be your enemy, the blow lands on yourself as well.

"Your Father wants you to show his love for your enemy through your behavior. I know this seems like a lot to ask. But stop and think: Does inflicting pain in retaliation heal the wound that you have suffered? Who will reach out to heal your pain when you, yourself, have helped create an atmosphere of conflict and mistrust? Will God do all the healing without any effort on your part? By no means! Does God not have the right to ask you first to set aside not just your weapon but also the anger that led you to pick it up?"

He told this story.

"Two neighbors argued persistently over a piece of property. Each was totally convinced that it belonged to him. One would fence the land off and put in a crop. The other would take the fence down and plow the crop under. Some seasons there would be an overwhelming growth of weeds, which each attributed to the malicious work of the other. While their land shared a common boundary, their animosity knew no bounds.

"One day the wives of the two men arranged to meet in secret. Neither was pleased with her husband's anger. Both were sad and disappointed that they were not able to be friendly and supportive neighbors. 'Suppose,' one proposed, 'that we were to cede our claim to the land to you in return for some payment that would fairly reflect the possibility that our claim may be, after all, legitimate.' Since neither wanted to continue the tension and hard feelings, the agreement was readily made. They quietly contacted an assessor and worked out what they considered to be a fair arrangement.

Only then did they tell their husbands about the agreement. And they insisted that their husbands endorse the plan.

"I do not need to tell you who in the story is God's collaborator."

9

Inn at Capernaum

It is now up to you to decide what, if anything, is appropriate for you to do for your brother.

Today I had the privilege of joining Jesus and his friends at the end of their day. The crowd had seemed unusually large and friendly, and Jesus was enjoying himself. There was some playful back and forth with some of the regulars. Now he was relaxing back at Zenoff's with a cup of wine and a sweet pastry Zenoff's wife had made. Several times now I've sat with them as they reviewed what had happened during the day. Their gathering doesn't seem to be organized in any way. Simon and Andrew and James and John have been there each time I have. Other than that the group seems to change from one occasion to the next. Andrew invited me today, but I think some people just tag along when Jesus leaves the lake.

John, the one Jesus calls Thunder Two, complimented him on the story he told today of the renegade son. The young rebel left home and squandered half of his father's wealth—what would have been his inheritance. Then he fell on hard times and went back home. His father, to the dismay of his older and more stable brother, welcomed him and gave a big party for him.

"Thanks," Jesus told John. "I think this story makes the point even better than the shepherd going after the lost sheep. It's easier for people to identify with the young rascal than with the sheep."

"That's certainly true of me," one of the men said. I think it was the tall one they call Philip. "I find it reassuring that this father is willing to forgive and forget and give us a chance to start over.

And he doesn't do it in a grudging way. Instead it's a family reunion. That's powerful!"

Then Simon said, "I was wondering where the story was going with the older brother. And then it just suddenly stopped."

Jesus said, "Did it need to go somewhere?"

"Not really, but it would have been interesting to know what happened!"

Simon is stocky with dark eyes under bushy eyebrows. He is balding on top and has a great, black beard that is showing speckles of gray. His fishing chores have put distinctive muscles on his shoulders and arms. He has a commanding stature. Were it not for the presence of Jesus, you would pick Simon out as the leader of the group. But he has at the same time an ingenuousness about him that prompts him to speak his mind with a disarming candor.

Now Jesus' eyes twinkled. "I have to be careful not to become just a storyteller or a wonderworker, an entertainer," he said. "I'm satisfied that the story made the point. But if you're interested . . ." Jesus leaned into the group and his voice became lower, conspiratorial—"here is the rest of the story."

The side conversations in the inn suddenly ceased, and you could feel the expectation in the group.

"The older son didn't enjoy the party," Jesus said. "He came to it briefly to be polite but found an excuse to leave early. He'd never liked his brother's friends anyway; they were rowdy, not his type. After that day of the party, life went on, and as was the bargain, the younger brother worked with the hired hands. He slept in his old bed and ate at the family table, but otherwise he did his work each day, got paid like the other day laborers, and was accorded no further favors.

"In time, due in part to the younger brother's work, the value of the farm increased until it was far beyond what it had been when their father had cashed half out to give to his rebel son.

"One day the rebel brother told his father and brother that he planned to leave again. This time, however, his was a mature, responsible decision. He was going to marry and set off on his own. He wanted his father and brother to know how deeply grateful he was that they had taken him back in when he was homeless and hungry. The younger son explained that he would visit from time to time, hold them always with affection in his heart, and bring grandchildren back to know their kin. With that he went off to pack."

Jesus was now speaking directly to Simon, who was listening intently.

"The older brother looked at their father and said, 'He really has changed, and he has worked conscientiously, helping to vastly increase the value of our farm. Perhaps we should give him something to help him get started, to thank him for his work here, and to wish him well in his new marriage.'

"'Your brother has already received his share. The farm and all of this is yours, remember?' the father responded. 'It is now up to you to decide what, if anything, is appropriate for you to do for your brother.'"

The group was silent, expecting a resolution. But Jesus was finished with the story.

After another moment, Simon grinned and said, "I should have left it alone! Now I'm wrestling with a bigger dilemma than I had in the first place."

Jesus laughed and excused himself to spend time alone.

❈10❈

Jairus's Daughter

Be a good father to those beautiful children.

Jesus has been away for a week or so. Word is that he has gone into the Decapolis to preach in the towns there. Tonight, for no reason, I walked down to the lake. There I found John sitting on a stone by the shore, lost in thought. He returned my greeting and invited me to sit with him.

"I take it he has returned," I said.

"Yes, just a little while ago."

"You look very weary. Was it a difficult trip?"

John seems a bit of a contradiction to me. He is slight in build and owns an engaging smile that makes him a favorite of everyone. Somehow he manages to be always close to Jesus, hanging on his every word. On the occasions when I have joined the group at the inn, he rarely comments. When he does, it is always to compliment or agree with whoever the speaker may be. He seems to be a favorite of Jesus' who perhaps sees in him a model of many of the virtues he preaches about. But on a couple of occasions John has—and rightly so—shown his temper to people who have been out of line and rude to others in the crowd at the lake.

"The trip wasn't especially difficult," John said. "He's remarkable. I'm just thinking about where all of this leaves me. I love him more than a brother, but I don't know what to do with all of this."

I said, "He's having the same affect on me. I listen to him and then I find myself searching for the meaning in my life. It would be easier if he simply gave us more rules to live by—and he does set higher standards for us—but there's something else . . ."

"He's trying to teach us how to love God," John stated. "But not just as Lord over all of heaven and earth. He calls God 'Papa,' and he wants us to feel that close to God, too."

We sat quietly for a while. The moon reflected on the water, and a soft breeze off of the lake washed over us.

"You were in the Decapolis?" I asked finally.

"Yes."

"What was the highlight?"

"He raised a young girl from the dead."

I bolted to attention and searched John's face and posture for some clue that he was joking. But he was quite serious. "How did it happen?"

"Well." He seemed almost reluctant to continue. "Maybe he didn't really raise her from the dead, but they thought she was dead." Then John told me this story.

It happened two days ago, at about midday. The father came out looking for Jesus. His name was Jairus. He is head of the synagogue in one of the towns. Jesus had met him on an earlier trip and liked him. "He is an honest man, a man with no guile," Jesus told us afterward. "He loves his people, and they care for him in return."

In any case, Jairus found us on the road and told Jesus that his daughter was gravely ill. He begged Jesus to come for her. As we approached the town after an hour's hurried walk, some of Jairus's people met us to report that his daughter had died. Jairus broke down in tears, begged Jesus to pray for him, and apologized for bringing him for no purpose.

Jesus put his hand on Jairus's shoulder and said, "No, no. She may be unconscious but she is not dead. We must go to her."

A number of people had made the trip with us but when we arrived at the house, Jesus took in only Simon, James, and me. The little girl was about twelve. Her mother and two young girls—sisters, I guessed—were at the bed weeping. Jairus broke into tears again and kissed his daughter's cheek.

Jesus took her limp hand and gripped it in both of his. He spoke briefly and sternly in a language that I did not understand. The girl stirred. There was a moment of enormous suspense. Then she opened her eyes and looked around at the people. The shock of what was happening stunned everyone to silence. Then her mother screamed and fell on her daughter with an embrace. The girl's eyes then met those of Jesus. He had the most gentle, happy look on his face.

"I'm Jesus," he said to the girl. "God sent me to make you better. How do you feel?"

Looking at him past her sobbing mother, she smiled weakly and nodded her head.

"What's your name?" he asked.

In a soft whisper she said, "Ruth."

"Ruth," he repeated. "What a beautiful name. What a great patron you have. You will grow up to be your own version of Ruth."

Now her sisters rushed to her. Her mother kept repeating her name, "Ruth! Oh Ruth!" When the mother finally stood again to look at Jesus, there was on her tearful face a look of mixed astonishment and relief. Words would not come; her lips moved but there was no sound. She shook her head in disbelief and spontaneously embraced Jesus. He looked so pleased for her.

When finally she caught her breath, Ruth's mother could only think to say, "You and your friends must stay for supper."

Jesus shook his head. "No, no. You have plenty to do here. Get this precious one something to eat because she is still weak." With that he left the house and we followed him. Jairus came out behind us, beside himself with joy and gratitude.

"God is pleased with you," Jesus assured him. "Now be a good father to those beautiful children."

"Do you think she was dead?" I asked when John finished the account.

John's eyes held mine. "Yes," he replied firmly. "She certainly looked dead to me. But either way, I'm sure we saw the power of God working through the Teacher. It is wonderful and humbling to be alive in this time and place."

It was getting late, and we walked back up the hill in the moonlight, each in his own thoughts. John said good night to me at the door to my place and moved on.

11

The Father's Children

We know that we belong to you more than
we do to the mother who bore us.

I went out to the lake again this morning to listen to him. The group was small and he was in a mellow mood. In some ways he is more interesting, more clever, more animated when the religious leaders are there to bait him and argue. John the baptizer was like that too. He was at his best when people tried to agitate him. But today Jesus had no enemies to deal with, and his speech was earnest but subdued.

He talked about the faithful love of the Lord for his children even in the face of failings. I thought he would retell the story of the father and his two sons but he did not. Instead he recalled how God had given a second chance to Adam, to Jonah, and to King David. He said he—Jesus—had come in a time when Israel was oppressed, not to create a military victory over Rome but to remind God's children of his care for them. This is care, he said, that transcends the political and economic circumstances of a time in history. Then he went on to talk about the Romans.

"The next Roman soldier that you see," he said to the group, "look carefully into his eyes. He has no need to hate you personally. He is a mercenary, remember, far from his home and the people he loves, earning an honest living in an occupation he understands probably as well as you know yours. His is an unpopular, even dangerous, livelihood that could snatch his years away at any time."

Jesus went on to say that the Roman soldier we next see is as much God's child as our own children. "Some people will be astonished in the kingdom of heaven to see the Roman soldiers they secretly despised sitting closer to the throne of God than they are."

The idea struck me as bizarre. We've been raised to see the Romans as the enemy, and their occupation of our land as a new Babylonian captivity. For us to see a Roman soldier as someone dear to God was a shocking suggestion. I could tell by the faces in the group around me that I wasn't the only one having trouble with the idea. But Jesus pressed on.

"Pagans, they say. Non-Israelites, they say. Hated Romans, they say." (I thought to myself that I have used those very words.) "And yet the Father who made both Roman and Jew," Jesus continued, "who *loves* both Roman and Jew, and who sees into hearts, knows that the Roman soldier who does his duty is closer to his kingdom than the priest or teacher—or any one of you, the 'chosen people'—who believes that your pedigree, your title, or your education automatically entitles you to a position of honor in my Father's house!"

His voice was quiet. But the earnestness in it struck at the root of my being. I may have imagined it but I sensed he was looking at me when he alluded to those with more education. I felt at once reassured and threatened. Am I too confident in God's approval? Does my life, my behavior, give me reason to know I am in God's favor? Or am I too impressed with myself and my talents? Most certainly I have always felt that I am better than the Roman soldiers. But now I wonder. And am I in danger of taking God's approval for granted while I neglect the people this Jesus advocates for: the poor, the widow, the outcast, those in prison? In my own heart I found his words disquieting.

At the end of his comments he invited us to pray with him. It is clear that this Jesus is a man of prayer. He is so comfortable with his God, his "Papa," that he must spend long periods of time with God, who is, for Jesus, a very personal deity. Jesus is a man at peace with himself, his preaching, and his role. I would say with his isolation also. He has his intimates. Some of them have become quite regular followers of his. I think Simon, whom he calls Rock, and Andrew are spending less time fishing and more time with him. I can't recall a time I've heard him when they were not there. The same is true of James, whom he calls Thunder One, and his brother John, Thunder Two.

But even when they are all there, he stands alone. He apparently has no wife, no children. He's distant from his family; some of his relatives think he's crazy and wanted to take him home. (Although lately I've seen James several times in the group by the lake.) And although he's not crazy, he is special in a way none of us can really name.

In any case, he invited us to pray with him this morning. His prayer went something like this.

"Father, our Papa, we trust your care for us. We know that we belong to you more than we do to the mother who bore us. Open our hearts to approach you more in love than in duty, more in trust than in fear. We come in confidence that you are a forgiving God, anxious to embrace us even after our betrayals. Let us follow your lead in this, forgiving those we consider to be our enemies and even—even!!—embracing as our brothers and sisters those we dislike or distrust."

I especially remember his repetition of the word *even*. He had prayed with his eyes closed, but at this point he looked around the crowd and engaged many eyes, my own included, after he spoke the word twice and before he finished the sentence.

Soon after that I was taken aback when, as he began to leave, he stopped in passing me and asked, "Soft Shoes, you are an educated man, are you not?"

I stammered that I had been taught to read and write, had furthered my education when I could, and had access to some written material.

"It is good," he said. "But that means that you have more responsibility than others."

The look in his eyes was both soft and challenging. I shall never forget it.

12

His Prayer

*The most beautiful flower has no color
without the light of the sun.*

I went to the lake this afternoon but he wasn't
there. I found Simon and Andrew and their
fishermen partners mending nets and getting
ready for a late afternoon trip out. I asked Andrew
where Jesus was, and Andrew said they thought he
was somewhere praying.

"Was he here this morning?"

"No. He's been gone two days." He saw my
questioning look and added, "That's not unusual.

He goes for two or three days and then just shows up like nothing has happened."

"Maybe he goes home to Nazareth."

"We don't think so. We think he just goes out to the desert and prays. Maybe he's found a place out of the sun where he talks to the Lord and listens. When we ask him about it, he just smiles at us and sometimes gives us one of those sayings that he often uses. He'll say something like, 'Without water, the horse cannot carry its rider' or 'The most beautiful flower has no color without the light of the sun.'"

"Does he eat cactus and bugs the way John did?"

"Don't know. I don't think he has the skills to know what he can eat in the desert, or how. I think he just fasts. We've noticed that when he's praying, he doesn't seem to know what's happening around him. It's like he's in another world." Andrew smiled a little. "Maybe he is."

"Does anyone go with him when he prays?"

"Not usually. Once or twice he's invited some of us to join him. But most of the time he disappears and shows up a few days later. So we wait. That's what we're doing now. We'll do some fishing and make a little money while he's gone."

With that Andrew left me and went back to his nets. And I went back to my shoes.

⁓13⁓

The Price of Choice

God has given us the ability to choose.

There was an interesting exchange at the lake today. Thomas, the one he calls South Wind, asked, "Master, if God cares about each of us so tenderly, then why is life so often made such a burden by other people?" It was not a hostile challenge like some of the leaders throw at him. The group that had gathered was attentive, and I could see that it was an honest question.

Thomas is by far the wittiest among Jesus' intimates. He is forever offering funny comments about the goings-on, even sometimes on the Teacher's own explanations and stories. He never spoils the point but sometimes his humorous observations have lightened up tense moments, especially in their conversations at the inn. His balding head makes him look older than I think he really is. But he is no buffoon. He'll often challenge Jesus with questions that strike me as truly profound.

Today Jesus responded to the query with a story, which is what he often does.

"A man made a wager with his neighbor," he said. "At stake were two rows of his vineyard. When the man lost the bet, the neighbor moved his fence to include the two rows in his own vineyard. Attempting to recover his loss, the man made another bet of two more rows. Again he lost the bet, and his neighbor moved the fence again. The man continued to wager until eventually he was reduced to his last two rows of vine bushes.

"Desperate, he went to his neighbor pleading that at least half of his vineyard be returned to him. 'Otherwise,' he pleaded, 'my family and I will have nothing to live on.'

"'Is that my concern?' the neighbor asked. 'Am I to have your family sit at my table and eat? You have made your choices and now it is your responsibility to live with them.'

"'I deserve to go hungry,' the man said. 'But my family has done no wrong. It is not fair for them to starve along with me.'

"'It was your responsibility to think of that before you made foolish wagers,' the neighbor responded.

"God has given us the ability to choose. The price of that freedom is that it is not just ourselves but others—often many others, including those we love—who must live with the consequences of our choices."

❈14❈

First Conversation

I must speak the message I was sent to give.

I had finished my work early and decided to go look for him at the lake. I put my tools and the shoes I'd just finished into the work cabinet. Then for a moment, standing at the door to my place, I looked back over it. It struck me as clean and comfortable. That's about how I see my soul as well. Perhaps too comfortable. But this Jesus is upsetting its tidiness. He is making me look with a fresh vision at what God wants from me.

I closed the door behind me and walked toward the lake. Passing through the village, I saw him sitting on the stone wall in the square all alone. Had there been no crowd today, or more likely, had he slipped away from them? I paused, confused.

He saw me and said, "Come sit with me, Soft Shoes."

I sat down next to him and for a few minutes we were silent. He seemed to be watching the pigeons walking around at his feet, pecking the stray seeds or scraps.

"Have you noticed the pigeons?" he asked. "They strut around in search of little morsels of food. They're always together but their work is individual. Somehow each one manages to find enough to survive for another day. There is something like that in what I am doing. You can see a loose solidarity in my followers. But each of them has his or her own life and responsibilities. They make what they can of each day and eventually they appear one by one before their judge."

I am often intrigued with his use of everyday things to see into more profound realities. Who bothers to notice the pigeons except occasionally as a nuisance? Now I had to gather my attention because he was pressing on with his thought.

"Sometimes I think that maybe what I demand is too hard on them. Perhaps I ask too much. They have enough responsibilities leading decent lives without being given extra challenges." He looked at me soberly. Then, no doubt seeing the puzzled squint on my face, he broke into a smile. "Do you think I could as reasonably ask the pigeons not to soil the ground?"

Then he spoke almost apologetically. "But I can't fail my Father. I must speak the message I was sent to give."

I said nothing. We sat in silence again for a bit. Then he stood and looked at me for a moment. "Yes," he said, "it is a good thing for you not to charge the widower." He turned and walked slowly away toward Zenoff's.

I had been pondering whether to charge for a pair of shoes I was making for a widower neighbor, and I'd almost decided not to charge him. But how could Jesus have known that I was wrestling with the question or how I had chosen to resolve it?

I returned to my shop, came inside, and sat down to think. Why did he speak with me? Should I be flattered? Is there something he senses in me that makes him feel that he can talk with me, even confide in me?

Then my thoughts turned to his message. Am I catching on? If I had to summarize it, how would I capture it? And who, really, has sent him? Is it the Lord I have grown up to know? And how did this commissioning take place? Jesus' candor makes him in many ways uncomplicated. But there is still much to his story I don't understand.

❦ 15 ❧

Birth of a Parable

If they do nothing about what they hear
and procrastinate in changing their lives,
then the message is wasted on them.

L ate yesterday I joined the group again at
the inn. They were having a discussion
unlike those I'd heard there before. Jesus
was concerned about the lack of urgency he sees in
the way that people take his message.

"I sometimes think they come to be enter-
tained," he said. "And I am not an entertainer. I'm
glad they've come." He slowly shook his head and
his voice picked up his frustration. "But if they do

nothing about what they hear and procrastinate in changing their lives, then the message is wasted on them." He looked around at the group. "I need a story that will make that point. Because now is the time and this is the opportunity for them to change the way they think and act."

The group took the implied challenge and began to wrestle with ideas and suggestions. I think it was Simon who suggested a story about women who are waiting for a bridegroom, fall asleep, and miss his arrival. The opportunity was there but lost. Somebody added the idea of including lamps. They run out of oil and that compounds their problem when they do wake up. Jesus got enthusiastic about this idea.

And today he used our bridegroom story but had further developed it to include five wise as well as five foolish women. I thought it was very effective. At least it moved me to be thinking further about my own life and priorities.

❧16❧

Scolding

The poor are yours. You cannot pretend otherwise.

He was angry today. I don't know what started it; I arrived late. Jesus and the others had been away for several days and it might have been something he saw or experienced in one of the other cities. But this scolding was eyeball to eyeball with the people of Capernaum.

"Shame on you!" he was shouting at us. "Shame on you!" He sounded like the Baptizer.

"Do you go to bed every night with a full belly while your neighbors are hungry? Shame on you!

"Are you warm and dry and oblivious to those who have no homes? Shame on you!

"Do you wish the widow well without asking how she will manage for herself and her children? Shame on you!

"Do you pay your help less than a fair share of your business profits and pride yourself that you have given them work? That is exploitation! Shame on you!

"Do you join the city's leaders in sweeping the poor and their problems out the door? And assume no responsibility for them? Shame on you!

"Time and time again God has sent prophets to tell you this. The poor are yours. You cannot pretend otherwise. The sick are yours. You cannot pretend otherwise. The widows are yours. You cannot pretend otherwise. The orphans are yours. You cannot ignore them. Those in prison are yours. You cannot pretend otherwise.

"Are you any better than those who heard the words of Elijah or Jeremiah or Ezekiel? Are you better even than the Samaritans or the pagans of the north or from the east? You are certainly not better, and shame on you for that!"

There was fire in his eyes.

"God demands! God is not asking. God *demands!* Did you come here today expecting soft, reassuring words? I am sorry to disappoint you. But I do you no service to tell you about your compassionate God if you have no compassion in your hearts except for those to whom you choose to show it.

"God chooses!" he fairly shouted. "God chooses! It is your obligation to respond. You may walk away from this place this afternoon, but you are not free to walk away from these duties. When a judge passes sentence, there is no option for saying, 'I will not comply. I do not care for your sentence.'"

Jesus is cut from a different fabric than John was. Unlike John, you would not describe Jesus as forbidding. He is personable. He smiles. He banters and teases. Apparently he loves a party. He is warm and sensitive with individuals. He is approachable.

But some days he challenges the selfishness in us. On those occasions he is formidable.

After he spoke, I came directly back to my place. I'm sure there was no friendly relaxation with him at the inn this afternoon.

I sat in one of my comfortable green chairs to think about all Jesus had said. It occurred to me that the old green chair was a perfect symbol for my life: familiar, comfortable, safe. Is Jesus calling *me* to new obligations? To a shift in my patterns, my priorities, my safe lifestyle?

If he is trying to wake me up, he is succeeding.

❧17❧

Second Conversation

God will send another Advocate, a spirit who will speak to people's hearts as I have spoken to their ears.

I found him again this morning sitting alone on the stone fence in the city square. This time I invited myself to join him. "May I sit with you?"

It startled his reverie. "Of course." His tone was welcoming but his face registered sorrow.

"Where is everyone?" I asked.

"Working probably." He gazed down the main path that led in one direction to the inn, in the other to the lake. "I've been in the desert for a couple of days. They don't know I've returned."

"Why do you look so sad?" I wondered if I should ask such a personal question.

He didn't respond right away. Then he said, "It's spring. Look at how the trees are budding. I don't expect to see this another season."

Did he expect to die soon? I had nothing to say, and neither did he for several moments. Then he said, "I am going to Jerusalem for Passover."

"Do you expect that to be . . . dangerous?"

"My friend Nicodemus tells me he's heard stories. Both the governor and the high priest are afraid that some insurrection will rise around me. They don't want that to happen, and Nicodemus fears they will do whatever they must to head that off."

"They jailed John the baptizer. Will they do that to you?" I didn't give him time to answer, because my questions were multiplying. "What charge could they bring? You are a man of peace."

"They will make something up if they have to. Justice is not the issue. They're afraid."

"Stay here in Capernaum," I blurted. "People love you here."

"That's what Nicodemus urged me to do. But I have to go. It is what my Father wants. I can't bring a message to Israel and leave out Judea."

"What will become of your message if something happens to you?"

"That is in the Lord's hands. God will send another Advocate, a spirit who will speak to people's hearts as I have spoken to their ears. I know this to be so."

We listened to the noises of the city. A caravan came by, perhaps headed to Zenoff's just west of us.

"Don't say anything about this to the others," he said. "They don't need to worry or get involved in what the officials do in Jerusalem."

"I promise," I said meekly. And in my fear for him, I immediately regretted the promise.

❈18❈

Pagan Woman

*You have bested me with your wit and
persistence and, yes, with your faith.*

They had been away for several days again,
this time in the region of Tyre. I am
happy to have him back at our lake. My
days have come to revolve around his preaching.
When he broke to have lunch, I sat on the grass
with Thomas.

"What interesting things happened on your
trip?" I asked him.

"There was one incident you would have loved,"
he said. "A pagan woman, Greek, I believe, wanted

him to exorcise a devil that had overtaken her daughter. Jesus rejected her at first, telling her that his focus was on the people of Israel. She told him, 'I should have known. Your arms are too short!'"

"Your arms are too short?" I interrupted. "What did that mean?"

Thomas laughed. "It struck me, too, as a peculiar remark. But it did have the effect she wanted, I think. He said right back to her, 'My arms are long enough to feed with God's word those who sit at the table of Israel.' She countered, 'Are they long enough to feed also the pets who hang around under the table to beg?' She had spunk. I loved it!

"Jesus answered, 'Are you saying that you yourself are such a cur?' She grinned at him and said, 'You teach that God cares for the sparrows. Are the family pets beyond the reach of his interest?'

"Now Jesus was into it and he had a huge smile on his face, too. He said, 'You are by Jewish standards a pagan. Why would I share with you the bread intended for Israel?'

"'Families take care of their pets,' she said without even a pause. 'They even pamper them. And everyone says that mongrels are the best and most loyal!'

"By now we could tell that she'd won him over. 'You are wonderful!' he laughed. 'I have verbally sparred with the learned religious leaders and I usually win. But you have bested me with your wit and persistence and, yes, with your faith. You may go home to your daughter. You will find her cured.' The woman said no more but walked right up to him and gave him an affectionate hug. Then she turned and hurried off."

I thanked Thomas for sharing the story and told him I regretted missing so much when Jesus was away.

"There is such depth to him," Thomas mused. "I believe there is much about him that we all miss, even those of us who try to follow him everywhere."

"But he's glad you follow him everywhere. He even has nicknames for you—South Wind."

Thomas smiled. "I'm sure it's a sign of affection. But I have the feeling it's a warning too; sometimes I talk too much, more like hot wind than anything meaningful." He rose then, and I laughed at his comment. As he walked away, I wondered what other meaning might be behind "Soft Shoes."

I returned to my shop and stood in the doorway peering in. The place looked lived in but presentable. "Soft Shoes," I thought. When God invited Adam to name the animals, he gave Adam dominion over them. When a parent names a child or a child names a pet, a bond is created between them. Freedom gets traded for responsibility on both sides. Suddenly there is a mutual accountability. And now—even though it is just a nickname—Jesus has named me.

❧19❧

Justice and Mercy

*When you show mercy to someone else, it is
your own failings that you redeem.*

Today a judge engaged Jesus in a dialogue
on the balance of justice and mercy.

"Every day I make decisions that can
be very harsh," the judge said. "And while I pray for
the wisdom of Solomon, I never know whether my
decisions have been right. People's property, their
freedom, sometimes their lives hang in the balance.
Even when I think I know what is right, I look into
their eyes, and my soul balks at what effect my judgment will have on the one life they have to live."

Jesus expressed admiration and compassion for the difficult job that honest judges struggle to perform. Then he told a story about a master who mercifully forgave a servant's debt. However, when the master later heard that the servant did not show similar mercy to a fellow servant in a minor issue, he was furious and rescinded his prior merciful judgment.

"God expects you to show mercy according to the measure that characterizes his mercy to you. When you show mercy to someone else, it is your own failings that you redeem.

"No one suggests that you allow the thief to steal your children's bread from your pantry. God has no quarrel with locks! But after a deed is done and cannot be reversed, what attitude will you adopt toward the thief? Will you turn to hate and vengeance? When you do that, the original loss is compounded by the loss of your own dignity and peace of mind."

He told another story. "Two warlords held prisoners from each other's armies. One day, one of the warlords was incensed by a misdeed of one of the prisoners, so he ordered the man to be executed. Word reached the other warlord, and he retaliated by killing two of his prisoners. Angered by this response, the first warlord killed ten more prisoners. Each reprisal escalated until all of the prisoners on both sides had been murdered. With that the two warlords again went to war with each other and were, in the process, so weakened that a king from outside their country invaded and destroyed them both.

"Revenge achieves nothing, and the perceived satisfaction of having evened the score is, in the end, a bitter illusion. God has set the example for you in the stories of Adam and Eve, the adulterous King David, and the prophet Jonah, who was first reluctant and then arrogant. Behavior that is moved by mercy wins the blessing of God and makes the wisest of judges."

❧ 20 ❧

Generosity

*Do you think that your Father's generosity
to you will dry up?*

Today he was talking about generosity.

"If a man needs a dollar, give him two.
Do you think that your Father's generosity
to you will dry up if you are generous with others?
If someone needs your coat," he said, "give him
your shirt as well. Think what a happy day that will
make for him.

"If a carpenter cuts a board too long by mistake, there is the opportunity to fix the problem.
If, on the other hand, he cuts the board too short,

it becomes useless for his intention. If a builder buys extra supplies, he gives himself options and is assured that he can finish the work. If, on the other hand, he skimps on supplies, he risks not being able to finish the job.

"Don't try to be at once stingy and generous." He was earnest as he said this. "You've noticed that the tree produces thousands and thousands of seeds. Clearly they will not all take root and grow. But in this way nature and its Creator have assured that the tree will have offspring long after it is cut down. Take that as your model for generosity. And don't look for every penny to bring repayment in gratitude."

Today most of his speech was light and even playful. But the message was just as challenging and disquieting as usual. He left us with much to think about. I have always considered myself to be generous, but in the light of his message, I must admit that my generosity has been too carefully measured.

There is one regular whose name is Jude. He periodically circulates a basket for contributions.

Apparently he keeps a purse of funds that take care of their needs when they travel. Jesus wouldn't let him circulate the basket today. I think he was concerned that it would appear mercenary in light of his message about generosity.

I suspect that Jude is a scribe, although he's private and communicates little information about himself. He seems to be fond of Jesus and at times is quite enthusiastic for the kingdom of which Jesus speaks.

The practice of accepting offerings is reasonable and probably necessary, but I believe some of Jesus' intimates are uncomfortable with it. I think it is Jude himself rather than his purse that makes them uneasy. There's no evidence that he's dishonest. But since Jude is something of a loner, he doesn't appear to be accountable to anyone. Some offhand remarks that I've heard James make lead me to believe that Jesus' intimates think that he is too trusting and maybe a bit naive about Jude.

21

Blind Man

Is God in our debt that we have the right to
set out conditions for him?

I saw one of his wonders—I think.

At the beginning of the morning, a blind man was asking Jesus to give him his sight. The man was of slight build and appeared to be in his early thirties. Jesus instructed him to just sit down and listen. But his pleas were both loud and insistent and it took some stern language from Jesus to get him finally to sit. Jesus' remarks after that were soothing—generally about being grateful for our gifts and appreciating the presence of God in the world around us.

It had been a beautiful day, making it easy for us to be aware of God's care as Jesus spoke. He used the blind man as a model. He pointed out that this man had never been able to see. Even so, there are many things about the world and in the man's life that he can appreciate even without his sight. The man supported Jesus' remarks by describing some of the blessings in his experience despite his handicap. "But," he added for Jesus' hearing, "I would welcome the chance to praise God also for what I might see with my eyes!"

Then, earlier than usual, Jesus told the crowd to go home; he was finished for the day. Some of us—maybe twenty including his intimates—stayed around to see what would happen with the blind man. Jesus helped him up, took him by the hand, and leaving us behind at the shore, walked with him north toward the hills by the lake. We settled in, talking. I ate the lunch I'd brought, even though it was nowhere near noon yet.

We could still see Jesus and the blind man in the distance. They stopped and appeared to be talking. We could see Jesus put his hands on the man's face. Suddenly there was a scream, then a strange whoop from the blind man. He appeared to be dancing around while Jesus stood there. They talked a little longer and then they started back to where we were waiting. As they got close to us, the blind man—well, the man who had been blind—began to run toward us. He was grinning and shouting, "I can see! I can see!" When he got to us, he seized the first person he found standing—it happened to be Simon—and began dancing with him in a circle, sweeping him around and around in his exuberance. "I can see! I can see!"

When Jesus caught up with this joyous scene, he put his hand on the healed man to calm him. "Remember what I said," speaking as a parent might when cautioning a child.

The man answered, "I know. I'm not to tell everyone, not to make a big thing of it." He looked at Jesus with an almost pained expression. "But I can see now—after all this time!" Defensively he added, "These people were here. They already know what you did for me."

"I understand," Jesus said to him. "I know that you can't expect your family and friends and neighbors not to notice that you can see. But I want you not to broadcast it as the Teacher's wonder. Just tell them that we prayed together and that God blessed you with your sight."

The man looked around the group. "Can you imagine what it is like to see for the first time? What can you say to the physician who gives you sight? Sight!"

Then he turned back to Jesus and promised, "I will not brag about this. I will just tell them that God chose to give me my sight." With that he wrapped his arms around Jesus, gave him a huge hug, and left running toward the city. In a moment he stopped suddenly and turned around, calling to Jesus, "But I know what happened!" Pause. Silence. "And these people know what happened!" Jesus just continued to look at him with a serious expression. Then the man waved, turned, and began again to run.

When the man was out of sight, Simon said to Jesus, "Why would you not want him to tell anyone? I'd think you would want *everyone* to know. This is a wonderful thing! A feat like this would get their attention. Why would you want to hush it up?"

Simon stopped then, and we could tell that an idea was coming to him. "In fact, why don't you do this more often? That would bring the large crowds out here every day!"

Jesus answered. "Ever since I discovered that I have this gift of healing, I've found circumstances where it seems the right thing to do. But I am never altogether comfortable intervening in natural events. I am pleased for that man. His name is Joshua. His life will be richer, now that his eyes can see. But what does this do for God's kingdom?

"I don't want to be seen as a magician. I am not here to dazzle everyone with my healing power. What does that accomplish for the kingdom? I am here to speak God's message and to call people to his love.

"I know that there are those who expect that God's presence is announced by great wonders.

They think that unless the seas part, God is in hiding. How foolish! Did anyone hear me this morning? Who cannot see the power and beauty of God in a million things around us, from the great blue vault of this heaven"—his arms were extended to embrace the whole sky— "to the tiniest ant going about its work! Can you see the might of God in the power of this sea as we look at it, or does it need to go dry for people to listen and hear and believe?

"People who think, 'I will believe if God dazzles me with the mountain moving' are deluding themselves. Does it not tempt God to say, 'Here are the conditions under which I will accept you and your expectations for me'? Is God in our debt that we have the right to set out conditions for him? He has been generous—extravagant—in showing us the evidence of his might and wisdom as well as of his tenderness and beauty."

He paused and looked off in the direction where the blind man had now disappeared from sight. Then he looked around at us. Even Simon was silent. When Jesus continued, there was frustration in his voice.

"Tell me," he said. "If there were nothing here, would you be so presumptuous or so imaginative as to say to God, 'Prove that you care! Put over there a series of mountains. And put here a great sea. And fill the sea with fish so that we can eat and earn our livelihood providing food for others. Think about that! How petty it would be for God to say, 'Maybe if I do these wonders, people will come and listen and believe.' God chooses to put out his evidence and his invitation in his own way."

Then he asked, "Do you see why I do not want to build my mission around signs and what people might consider to be wonders? They await a champion who will dazzle and delight them. Or one who will hack down their enemies with a great sword. But I proclaim God's message as a prophet proclaims God's message. Those who choose to believe, choose to believe."

He was reading our hearts. I surely had been represented by Simon's challenge. Why does he work so hard to convey his message in words when he has the choice of just doing it with his wonders? But he is right, of course. I choose to follow him because of the truth that I hear in his message and because of the holiness that I see in his person and life. How would a hurricane of miracles alter that?

❧22❧

Jude

Every decision you make is shaped by the commitment to take my words seriously.

This is what Jesus was telling us this morning: "I'm sure that many of you see the path I lay out as wholesome and reasonable. But I will not mislead you. God does not sleep. What he requires is persistent and urgent. Our obligations to him are not satisfied with Sabbaths at the synagogue or feast times at the temple. True religion requires that everything you do and every decision you make is shaped by the commitment to take my words seriously."

He was interrupted at this point by a toddler who ran up and wrapped his arms around Jesus' legs. Relieved of the tension of the message, the crowd snickered. Jesus smiled and picked up the little man.

"What is your name, son?" he asked.

"Joseph," came the clear reply.

"That's a wonderful name. There is a man I admire very much. His name is Joseph, too." The boy beamed.

Still holding little Joseph, Jesus again looked at the crowd.

"Young Joseph's job is to be a child. He's already learned to walk and run and talk. His job is to play and learn and grow. It takes him all day every day." He looked at Joseph and asked, "Doesn't it?" They exchanged broad smiles.

"Joseph doesn't have a day to learn and a day to play and a day to grow," he continued. "It is all together, continuous. And what God wants of you is something like that. God's demands don't keep to a schedule. They are always there. As things happen and opportunities come along, he wants you to respond with care and sensitivity and gratitude and generosity."

At this point, he kissed Joseph on the cheek and set him down. The boy scampered back to his mother.

"I don't promise that this response is easy," he told us then. "But if it is beyond what you are willing to give, then you are not a disciple of mine no matter how attractive you may find my message."

When we stopped around noon, I met Jude, the one who sometimes passes the basket when Jesus preaches. Many of us bring something to eat when we go to the lake, and Jude sat down with me as I was having my lunch.

"You're the one he calls Soft Shoes," he said.

"I'm a cobbler in town," I explained. "I don't understand how Jesus knew that, but I'm glad that he's noticed me."

"He's an amazing man," Jude commented. "I still find it hard to believe that all of these people come to hear him. It's remarkable."

I said, "The religious leaders seem to be leaving him alone lately. There haven't been the confrontations that were so common during the early weeks of his preaching."

"I think it's the calm before the storm," said Jude. "I worry that they'll find a way to silence him. From their perspective, he's not good for business. At first, when he was reading in the synagogue and preaching, I believe they thought he was harmless and would go away if they exposed him. But the strategy didn't work. He beats them in all their arguments. He also makes much of their teaching look foolish. In the minds of the people, he's become the hero, and they are the villains. They think their quibbling is impressive scholarship, but he cuts right to the heart of the law. That's threatening their livelihood, and a man gets mean when you do that to him."

"Well, if they see him as a threat, then the large crowd won't help. He's not keeping a low profile."

"Precisely," Jude went on. "I don't know what their plan might be, but I'm sure that they feel it's necessary to do something. Throwing him out of the synagogue won't have any effect now; he seldom goes there anymore. And it's not like he's breaking any laws except some of the picky provisions of their code. There is nothing substantial they can charge him with. If you listen to him, it's clear that he's not inciting anyone to sedition. But I'm sure he makes them nervous."

"The rebellion he's calling for is in our individual souls," I said. "And that is war enough. I think I'm a better person for having listened to him. At the same time, I still haven't decided exactly who or what in my soul is the enemy."

"I'm having the same problem," said Jude. "I was really swept away with him at first. But now I have to wrestle with all of this. I'm a young man. If they jail or even kill him, where does that leave me?"

This sort of talk surprised me. The comment reflected a perception very different from mine. I looked into his eyes and thought I saw fear rather than excitement.

As if to confirm my unspoken thought, he said, "I'm no coward. But why would I want to end up dead or in jail because of my fascination with this Jesus? When enthusiasm and common sense collide," he finished, "a person has to be reasonable."

Suddenly I felt uncomfortable with this man. It struck me that his relationship with Jesus was too calculated. I find Jesus to be liberating. He makes me feel whole—challenged to be a better person, but whole.

And here was a man who'd heard what Jesus had just said about commitment!

I was relieved that I had finished eating and could excuse myself and leave him.

❦ 23 ❧

Moses and Elijah

*God's glory is not hidden. It's a gift he
wants to share.*

Word was that he was not at the lake
today. So I stayed at the shop and
worked. In the early afternoon, I was
sitting on the bench in the shade outside my shop
when three of his intimates came along from the
general direction of the lake. If they had been talking, I wouldn't have interrupted them, but they
were silent and looked thoughtful, almost sullen.

"Would you like to get in out of the sun for a
bit?" I called. "I could offer you some tea."

It was Simon and the two Thunders. They exchanged glances and promptly, without a word spoken, agreed to accept my invitation. I'm flattered that they're so comfortable with me. I don't think anyone would consider me an intimate of Jesus, but they all know me both by sight and by the name he's given me. And they consider me to be a disciple and friend of his movement. The three came in and sat down at my table, and I began to get the tea ready.

"You all look like you've seen a ghost," I said to break the silence. They did appear to be overserious and, for tanned outdoorsmen, even a bit pasty.

James broke into a grin.

James is the older brother of John. You wouldn't guess that, because his round face, tight curly hair, and stocky build all contrast with his brother. He has a quick temper, which shows especially when the pious ones attack Jesus. It's not unusual to see Jesus give James a quick, unobtrusive hand gesture to suggest, "Let me deal with this." I've often noticed James nodding in agreement when Jesus is making a point, even in their informal conversations at the inn.

"That's funny," James said, more to his companions than to me. Then to me he volunteered, "We think we did just see a ghost—or two really."

I froze, then slowly lowered myself into the fourth chair and waited for them to continue.

James and John deferred to Simon, who cleared his throat before speaking. "This morning he invited us up the mountain to pray with him."

John interrupted, looking sharply at Simon. "He told us not to say anything about it."

Simon is not easily moved from his opinions of what is acceptable and what is not. I think Jesus sized him up well when he chose the nickname Rock.

"Soft Shoes is one of us. He just happened not to be there."

"Be where?" I prodded.

"On the mountain with us," Simon went on. "He's often—well, at least several times—invited us to go up the mountain with him. When we get there, we pray. Well, he prays. Mainly, we watch. I think he hopes that we'll learn just from being with him during his prayer."

John added, "He does seem to find it helpful to have us there."

"Sometimes I think that his conversations with his father are difficult for him. So we believe that he wants us there while he gets started." That was James. Clearly they've discussed this more than once among themselves.

Simon continued. "Today he was sitting on an outcropping of rock. We've gone there with him before for his prayer. He closed his eyes as he usually does. Gradually we noticed that there was a glow around him. It was as if his holiness was outgrowing his body and had a presence of its own."

"Yes, that's a good way to describe it," James said. "We all saw it. I think we were all a little scared."

"More than 'a little scared,'" John picked up. "You were terrified, Simon; I saw your face."

"Then," Simon continued, ignoring John and caught up in trying to explain the event, "there were two more . . ." He paused to find the right word. ". . . presences. They were on the rock with him, on either side of him."

"And they were talking with him but it was like a dream—we couldn't tell what they were saying," said John.

"But we are convinced that they were Moses and Elijah, right there with him in his prayer. And talking with him," Simon said. "And he was talking with them. We could hear them but we couldn't understand what they were saying."

"It was our Jesus," James broke in. "And he wasn't just with them; he was the *center* of it all! Our Jesus!"

I've realized since then that they were like three excited little boys who had experienced a very special event together and were tripping over each other to relate the story. I was lucky enough to be the first friend that they had the opportunity to tell! The tea water had heated, but I sat transfixed with the story. No one was thinking about tea. Simon picked up the story again.

"Then we all got the same message. We can't decide whether it was a voice, a fourth voice, or an intuition or revelation of some kind. The message was that this Jesus is the presence of the Lord with us. This is not just an angel sent with a message from God. Nor is he just a prophet commissioned to deal with us on behalf of the Lord. This somehow *is* the presence of God among us."

"Like Moses with the burning bush," I reflected.

"Yes," said John. "We were really frightened. It was there!"

"And brave old Solomon here" —John was smiling now at Simon— "says, 'Let's build a shrine here for Jesus, Moses, and Elijah.'" He looked at Simon, teasing.

John's humor had relieved the tension some. "Look who's talking," said Simon. "You were frightened to the point where you couldn't talk. I was at least able to say something."

"We were all frightened," said James. "We have no idea how long this lasted. Eventually everything was normal, and Jesus was there, and he had finished praying. Then he looked at us and said, 'God's glory is not hidden. It's a gift he wants to share.'"

"We came down the mountain with not much to say." It was Simon again who spoke. "Jesus didn't say any more about it. And by then he was back to normal—no glow or voices. We were each alone with our thoughts, and it wasn't until he left that the three of us began to talk about this."

John looked at me and said, "He did tell us not to discuss this with people. We probably shouldn't be talking about it now."

"I will keep the confidence," I promised. No one knew what to say after that. Finally, I asked, "Do you want the tea?"

Simon spoke for the group. "No. But thanks. And thank you for listening to us. An experience like that is hard to keep in. It's, well, something like steam from a teakettle!"

"You're learning to talk like him," I said. They laughed and left. And here I am with my thoughts about him.

Could they have imagined it? That strikes me as unlikely. These are three tough men, full of life experiences. Not the type to have their imaginations run away with them.

I've been wondering if this has been happening often to Jesus but, until now, without the witnesses. What was being said? Were these otherworldly presences just reassuring Jesus? Or were they perhaps coaching him? Is it possible that the message he preaches and the stories he tells are revealed to him by the Lord himself, communicated to him through his prayer?

There is so much of this that is beyond me.

⸻24⸻

Riches

*Each of you must look into your heart and
understand what generosity God requires
from you.*

There was an interesting discussion today
between Jesus and a young man in the
crowd. The man asked him, "Just tell me
clearly: what does God want from me?"

Jesus countered, "Moses gave you the plan
when he brought the commandments to you.
Don't kill, don't steal, honor your parents, don't
lie, don't commit adultery. That's a very big order.
Do all these things, and God will be pleased with

you. You didn't expect a new, special set for you, did you?"

"I was taught all that from when I was a small boy," the man responded. "Surely you have something more demanding to suggest. I am a successful and wealthy man. I could be reaching out in some way. But I'm paralyzed with indecision about where to begin using my energy and wealth."

"So you want a challenge," Jesus said.

"Yes. I want something that will let me make a difference. I thought you could offer me guidance, advice."

"Give it all away," Jesus said. "Give it to the poor. It doesn't matter exactly how you do it; just get rid of it. And then join me. Commit your life to helping me preach and spread this good news. I have colleagues here. Join us."

The man was dumbstruck. "Just give it all away? It doesn't matter how? I'm thinking of using some of my resources to be helpful to someone. But I don't know about this."

"I'm answering your question," was Jesus' comment.

"That I've got to think about," the man said. And then he drifted away. Jesus watched him go and then returned to his discourse. But it was only a few minutes until he returned to the incident.

"That rich young man is generous," Jesus said. "He apparently leads a good life. And he has resources and is willing to share them. But not all of them. He's not willing to give up his security for the kingdom of God.

"And it's not always money, is it? People are wealthy in different ways. Some have a wealth of talent or skill or experience. But unless they have a mind-set of generosity, they will measure out what they are willing to give away. Only when they are willing to part with all of it do they give God credit as the source of their wealth and talent. Generosity starts when a person gives up control of wealth and security and chooses to depend on God. People might say with their mouths that they trust God or that they recognize that their wealth, whatever form it comes in, is from God. But they balk when it comes to trusting him entirely for tomorrow's needs."

As he often does, Simon spoke what was on all of our minds. "Isn't it prudent for us to keep what we need for ourselves and our families?"

Jesus answered, "Those are choices you must make. But do you see my point? You say, 'I believe in a provident God who has the means and the will to take care of me. But I will hold something back in case God isn't there for me.' What you hold back becomes your insurance in case your trust in God is misplaced. By your actions you are saying, 'I trust God as long as I'm still sure I can take care of myself.' What kind of faith is that?

"See," Jesus continued. "Wealth in its various forms becomes a weight that can hold you down. If you cannot let go of it, you'll find it hard to reach for the kingdom. You become trapped by the things of earth—things that preoccupy your mind and time and energy. Then pursuing God and his kingdom become lower priorities and lesser issues.

It is hard—naturally hard—for the rich person to let go, to get untangled from the stuff of wealth.

"The poor have little to hold on to, and so, for them, it is in some ways easier to let go on behalf of God's kingdom. But the rich have much to hold them and to engage their hearts. For them, holding fast to the kingdom is much, much more difficult."

"Are you saying that the rich young man is damned?" asked Simon.

"He is hearing the challenge to do more with what he has," said Jesus. "He has a generous soul. But he still wants to measure his generosity, doesn't he, and not risk the security that his wealth gives him.

"The lesson in this incident is for you. Each of you must look into your heart and understand what generosity God requires from you."

He told this story. "A man had great wealth, but it never seemed enough for him. He rejected many opportunities to be helpful to his widowed sister-in-law and her children. 'Some day I will have enough,' he rationalized. 'Then I will help take care of them. But not yet.'

"One day he set out on a long trip by sea. To prepare, he changed his treasure into two hundred gold coins and put them in a money belt that he wore around his waist under his tunic." Out at sea the ship took on water and sank. The crew and passengers clung to floating debris for several hours until another ship found them and brought them to safety. But the rich man, burdened with the weight of his gold coins, was unwilling to cut them loose and sank in the sea and drowned.

"So tell me. What was the value of his gold— and for whom was it valuable—as his fortune lay with him on the ocean floor?"

Here is a footnote to the discourse. Jesus refused to allow Jude to pass his basket through the crowd. Whenever he touches on generosity, he apparently worries that any collection will somehow compromise or diminish the power of his message.

~25~

Zacchaeus's Conversion

When God forgives, his forgiveness is
coming from nerve and sinew.

I want to get this down before I lose the details. This morning, several of us, Jesus included, arrived at the lake early, before the crowd. Jesus became engaged in this conversation with Simon and Andrew.

"How was the dinner with Zacchaeus?" Simon asked.

Zacchaeus is a tax collector, known in the area but not respected. We've all considered him to be dishonest. Yesterday the crowd was large, and

Zacchaeus had climbed a tree to see Jesus more easily. Jesus startled everyone by stopping to speak with him, and before the conversation was over, Jesus had invited himself to dinner with Zacchaeus.

"You missed a great meal, Rock," Jesus said. "He prepared a huge feast."

"What did you have?"

"He must have some wonderful friends or connections to do all this on such short notice," Jesus said. "He had lamb, roasted, with a variety of trimmings and a delicious red wine. The Thunder brothers and Philip joined me. It's too bad you couldn't come."

"We decided to do some work," Andrew explained. "You left early enough for us to have some good daylight time."

"Work is good," Jesus said, a humorous glint in his eyes. "You're sure you weren't just embarrassed to accept an invitation from the likes of Zacchaeus?"

"You should have heard people talk after you left," said Simon. "The teachers at the synagogue don't think much of your partying with sinners, and they consider Zacchaeus to be a sinner—you know the rumors of his dishonest dealings."

"They don't think much of my partying with anybody, do they? In their minds, parties and piety don't mix."

"Zacchaeus was really excited that you were willing to go and have dinner with him," said Andrew. "He seemed genuinely committed to doing the right thing."

Jesus said, "I think he's sincere. But conversions of heart need to be followed up on. Goodness is a mind-set that drives not just one decision but choice after choice."

Simon said, "But Zacchaeus promised you that he would return fourfold whatever he had cheated people out of. That sounds very genuine and generous to me."

"The intent is generous indeed, Rock. I'm sure that Zacchaeus meant what he said yesterday. But will it happen? And even if Zacchaeus follows through on his promise, such a conversion does not make the prior pain go away. Zacchaeus is sorry for having cheated people, but he can't fix the wrongs by being sorry or even by trying to make it up to those wronged. The deeds have lasting effects. The pain stays.

"Sin is an enormous thing. So, in a way, I can understand the harsh judgment of our pious friends. But they have only a superficial appreciation of the malice of sin. To understand the breadth and depth of what sin does—to innocent people, to relationships, to the community, even to the sinner—is beyond their comprehension. But even so, they are not nearly as willing as the Lord is to forgive and move beyond the damage that evil causes.

"When God forgives, his forgiveness is coming from nerve and sinew. It is like an embrace given to a villain who has gravely injured someone you love."

There was a moment of silence. Jesus is fascinating when he becomes engaged in a theme like this. There is a conviction, a passion about the way he speaks, even the gestures he makes. He looked around and then smiled the way he does sometimes when he realizes how wrought up he's become.

"So where does that leave Zacchaeus?" asked Simon innocently.

"I'm happy with his conversion. I was happy to give him God's embrace of forgiveness. It was fun to join his party celebrating his new start. Can you think of anything that more deserves a party?"

By then the crowd was gathering, and Jesus stood to get ready to speak with them.

❦26❧

Marriage

*The world of earth and flesh bears testimony
to the world of spirit.*

Today, late in the afternoon, Jesus sent the crowd home early after his preaching. He, most of his intimates, and a few others of us stayed for a while at the lake. We relaxed in the pleasant weather, watching puffy clouds drift over the water.

"You never got married," Simon said abruptly, turning to Jesus. "Tell us about that."

My stomach turned into a knot! That's quite a personal question. I had wondered about this—I think all of us had—but would never have asked. Simon has a way of asking my questions for me.

Somehow I could never imagine John the baptizer as married. I had only seen John twice, but I couldn't imagine anything like a romantic side to him. Jesus, on the other hand, is sensitive and balanced. He has women friends, and there are many women in his daily audience. If he were not so absorbed in his "Father's work" I could see him married and bringing up children. But he's never mentioned the subject, not even in the informal conversations at Zenoff's.

"Most of you are married," Jesus said. "Would I be foolish enough to suggest it's a bad idea?"

"But if it's a good idea," Simon persisted, "then why not for you?"

"The marriage relationship is beautiful. Don't you appreciate seeing whole families at the lake? The men and women are wonderful support to each other. And that's as it should be. 'Male and female he created them,' remember? And as God intended, marriage provides a home where children can be born and raised. Simon, you know how important your marriage is to your being who you are."

"Jesus, you must tell that sometime to my wife!" Simon quipped.

"Be careful," Jesus said, "or I'll tell her a whole lot more!"

It was good fun and it relieved the tension of Simon's original question. But now Jesus turned serious. "I have not married because of what my mission requires. There are two worlds. One is the world seen and felt and tasted and heard. This is the world of earth and flesh. The other is the world sensed and believed. This is the world of spirit and faith. I've come not to dismantle that first world but to bring focus to the second world.

"God is in the world of spirit. So how does he reach into the world of earth and flesh? How does he communicate with his human family? How does he reach across that gulf between earth and spirit? How can he awaken his children to that world on the other side, on his side? Creation itself bears his mark. It is possible to know something of the artisan by looking at his handiwork. The flowers, the birds, the thunder, the sea—they preach more eloquently than I can. You have heard me borrow them to make my points. So the world of earth and flesh bears testimony to the world of spirit.

"Beyond those things, God sends his prophets. Throughout the story of Israel, the prophets have borne his message, asking his people to reach deep into their souls where *their* spirit finds the spark of *his* spirit."

Simon interrupted. "So does earth get in the way of spirit?"

"It can, but it doesn't have to and was never meant to," Jesus continued. "Earth and flesh become the sisters of spirit. John, remember, used water as the midwife for the spirit. Water for him celebrated the point where earth and spirit met in the lives of his audience. The risk you referred to, Simon, does happen when earth and flesh so absorb someone that he or she forgets and neglects spirit. It is like day and darkness. There is nothing wrong with darkness. In fact, the night invites cool and rest. But if the day is also night, then the beauty and potential of the sunlight is lost and the earth—or soul—dies.

"My work is to show people the sun. For me, being married might compromise the time and energy I could give to the mission God has given me. My mind and heart can focus on only this mission."

"Besides, you're a nomad," Thomas quipped. "If she traveled with you, she'd have a husband without a home. If she stayed in one place, she'd have a home without a husband. And those times when you did come home, you'd just slip out to go pray in the rocks!"

Jesus likes Thomas's sense of humor. Besides, Thomas had a good point. There are several women in the group who, I'm sure, would gladly respond to a marriage arrangement with Jesus, and then discover that being married to an itinerant preacher is a bad prospect!

27

The Storm

It is good to be with friends.

All the talk among the crowd today was that Jesus had walked on the water of the lake. The rumor was that some of his intimates had gone out in the boat late the day before yesterday. Jesus apparently walked out to them across the water and came back in the boat with them. When Jesus took a break from talking to us this morning, I sought out Andrew and asked him what there was to the story.

Andrew said that the story is true, although Jesus had asked them not to talk about the incident.

Someday I'm going to get into trouble pressing them for information that's supposed to be confidential. But the truth is that they love to talk about it, and I don't think Jesus really minds if they talk to me. Since our two conversations in the town, I have the sense that he trusts me.

"We were going to go to Bethsaida because he'd planned to preach there yesterday. He'd told us to go ahead, that he would find a way to get there by himself. There are several other people in his crowd who have boats, so we weren't concerned that he'd find a way. So we left him there and started out in the late afternoon. There was some wind, but we didn't expect any problems. Then a storm closed in on us, and the going got rough very fast. We weren't making much headway, and we were taking on water."

I could tell from Andrew's face as he was relating the story that the storm had frightened them. It takes a lot to scare these seasoned fisherman—they've ridden out many storms on that lake.

"We had been out for an hour or so," Andrew continued, "and we were getting tired. Then Simon pointed to something out on the water. At first we weren't sure what it was, but it looked like a person was walking toward us! We watched for a few minutes while we wrestled with the boat—no one saying anything. Finally Simon shouted, 'I think it's Jesus!'"

I asked, "What was he doing there? I thought you said he had stayed behind on shore when you went out."

"We don't know. No one could remember exactly where he was when we left.

"In any case, after a few more minutes, we could all tell that it really was him. As he came closer, he didn't say anything. We probably looked peculiar, all of us on the same side of the boat now with our mouths open and our eyes popping—the wind whipping the boat around. Jesus was thrashing through the water, looking like a man climbing a rocky mountain path in a driving rain. He was not looking at us, and for a moment, he appeared to be about to pass us. Simon called to him, and he looked at us as though he'd been interrupted in a task and then shouted 'Hello.' With some effort he came over to the boat and we helped him in. He was drenched. None of us knew what to say. It was Simon who shouted over the wind, 'This is a bad one—I'm afraid we're losing the boat!' Don't you love Simon? Jesus has just walked across the water, and Simon's talking about his boat!"

"So what did Jesus say?"

"Nothing that would explain what had just happened. He said, 'It is good to be with friends.' It was as though people take a stroll on the sea all the time. But he sat down and made a gesture, and the storm stopped. The wind backed off to a breeze and the waves dropped. We were exhausted by then and decided to come back here. We finished the trip easily."

"What do you make of it?"

"Sometimes I make perfect sense of him," Andrew said. "At other times I don't think I know him at all. I'm grateful that he walked on the water—we might all be dead if he hadn't. But who knows what really happened or what it means?"

"Does he use this sort of miracle to prove to us that his message truly has the endorsement of the Lord?"

Andrew shrugged. "That doesn't make sense when you see how he fights being known as a wonderworker or a magician. He wants his message to be taken on its value without the intimidation of signs and wonders."

"Yes, but many times it's as if he can't help himself. He does these wonders and then orders people not to tell anyone."

"I know. There's a spontaneous streak in him. He does things and then he seems to think, 'Oops. I didn't mean to do that.' Maybe that's what happened that night. It could be that he just decided to take a walk in the storm and then stumbled into us. Or maybe he got to worrying about our trip and went looking for us. And you're right; he did tell us not to discuss this."

"You have to consider," I said, "that maybe everything he does has a plan. He doesn't want to show his power over nature in front of the crowds because of the spectacle it would cause. But he wants people closer to him to understand that he has that power."

Andrew nodded. Then another thought came to me, an unpleasant one, but I had to speak it.

"Especially if he expects to be jailed . . . or killed . . . he wants you and the others to be sure of who he is and what his mission is, so that you won't doubt him when the time comes."

"You may be right. I've thought about that, but I can't see any of us taking his place—as a preacher or a wonderworker. Well, Simon and James might speak in front of a crowd. But the healings, the exorcisms, the other miracles . . .

"Let's just say this," Andrew continued. "A year or so ago I had no special preoccupation with God. Since meeting Jesus, I have to confess that my life is consumed with God, the father whom Jesus talks about so affectionately. And while I don't see myself as having the skills or commission to speak for him, I do have the enthusiasm to want to share him with others."

I knew exactly what he meant.

"What would you do if he died?" I asked.

"I've chosen not to deal with that question. As long as he's around, I'm fine with how this is working for me. If that changed, I don't know how I would handle it." He looked at me wistfully. "I'm a coward."

"Aren't we all," I replied.

~28~

War

If you remember that your enemy is also God's child, then you will hesitate to take what you call justice into your own hands.

Today at the lake Jesus was challenged by a large muscular man who I'm sure was a Roman and probably a Roman soldier. There was no sword or spear or helmet to identify him, but his speech and manner suggested that he certainly was not anyone from the area around Capernaum.

"Teacher," he said, "you have told these people that they should be peacemakers and give a man their shirt also if he demands their coat, or walk two miles if he demands one from them. Then what do you say to them if that man demands that they should take up swords to throw off what he considers to be injustice and oppression?"

The question was clearly intended to put Jesus on the spot. I wondered immediately whether the burly man had been sent by some authorities to set a trap or at least to create an awkward dilemma for Jesus.

Jesus didn't hesitate. "Scripture says there is a time for war and a time for peace. There is a time to take up the sword and a time to lay it down. It is the wise man who knows which time is which. You know that from the time of Cain and Abel, men have fought for false issues, imagined injustices, and causes that are not worth the cost in blood."

A tall thin man with a neatly groomed beard interrupted from the crowd to shout angrily at the Roman for Jesus to hear. "But you are outsiders who have come into our land and taken over. That surely deserves some response to throw off this injustice!"

The Roman shouted back, "Without the might of Rome here, you people would have anarchy! It is Rome that provides you with peace. It is Rome that provides you with roads and water and protection. It was Rome even that built you your precious temple in Jerusalem."

"Go back to Rome and send us a bill for the temple," the tall man fired back. "We will easily pay it from the money you take away from us in taxes."

A murmur went through the crowd. We had no idea what rank this Roman might have or whom he might be representing. So the man's outburst struck me as quite foolish.

I looked at Jesus. "*You* didn't create the situation," he said, pointing at the Roman, "and *you* can't make it go away," he continued, pointing now at the angry Galilean. "But that doesn't stop you both from venting your anger on each other.

"Peace in the end comes from the hearts of people. When people are willing to care about each other, understand each other's needs and issues, and forgive past grievances, then peace is possible, no matter what the starting point may be."

The word *peace* has an attractive sound. But if the price is forgiving past grievances, it is no wonder that we find it so elusive.

"God wants his children—all of his children—to be free," Jesus continued. "But ambition and political motives often lead people of power to enslave others. Before God, there will be a day of reckoning for those people.

"But in the meantime, think about this. You protect your possessions as though they were truly yours. You say, 'This is my land,' and God laughs. He says, 'Did you make the land? Did you put its richness there? Did you cause the rain to water it?' And yet if someone encroaches on it, you feel justified to defend it with your sword. And then God weeps.

"If someone inflicts on you an injury or an injustice, does that give you the right to punish as though you were the Lord? If you remember that your enemy is also God's child, then you will hesitate to take what you call justice into your own hands."

The crowd was now for the moment sheepishly silent, including the two antagonists in the group.

Jesus looked at the Roman who had posed the original question. "I have no quarrel, my friend, with a government, or a soldier, who does the job necessary for keeping the peace. But this service must be given with respect and restraint. Wars and insurrections designed to seize or expand power are wrong. Wars and insurrections designed to avenge real or imagined wrongs are wrong. The harmony that God intended has, from the beginning, been undermined by the greed and ambition and pride of sinful men. And tell me, who among you can claim that he is blameless? Who among you has not struck out in anger or cheated or placed your own interests above your good judgment of what is right?"

He raised both arms for emphasis. "And *nations* suffer from the same faults as individuals. They embrace goals or causes for self-interest and impose their will, if they can, on others."

I saw the Galilean glare at the soldier. Clearly he was ready to blame Rome, but I doubt he was ready to take any personal responsibility for conflict.

Then Jesus turned to the rest of us. "From time to time in the past, God has raised up prophets and kings to reestablish the identity or security of his people. But which of you has he anointed to take that responsibility upon himself today? Which of you has he authorized to make widows and orphans in a cause that you have somehow determined is just?"

"Are you saying that we must wait for God to intervene?" asked the tall Galilean. "How long must we wait for God to send us a new king to free us from Rome?"

Jesus looked at the man steadily. "What if God is more interested in the freedom each of us must experience in our own hearts? What if God really wants not to set one nation against another but to bind all nations together under his love and care?"

I could tell by the looks on faces all around me, that this idea was hard to digest. We have always been the *nation* Israel, united under God of our forefathers. Would Jesus have his own nation dismantled? What was he saying?

"Remember this," he said. "In past times God raised his arm to free his people from the oppression of the Egyptians and then of the Babylonians. But do you think that for all those years of captivity his love did not continue to embrace each and every life?"

After this I watched the Roman drift away without a word. Anyone who was digging for evidence of treason in Jesus' preaching had to be disappointed on this day.

But I think others were disappointed, too. We had begun to hope that Jesus was the long-awaited liberator. Perhaps he is, but he will not liberate us as we have imagined. Jesus fills me with great hope, and at the same time he dims other hopes I have cherished.

29

Confrontation

Is God constrained to speak only in thunder
and lightning as he did on Mount Sinai?

The leaders from the synagogue showed up this morning to challenge Jesus. There were four of them; maybe they think there is safety in numbers. When they interrupted, Jesus was talking to the crowd about God being his father and ours.

"This is blasphemy, what the man is saying! This is not a meaningless relationship like we are all children of Abraham and therefore wards of the

Lord. He is speaking as though God is his physical father. Surely you all see how absurd this is!"

They were speaking to the crowd but, of course, for his ears. And the crowd ratcheted up their level of alertness and waited for Jesus to respond.

"Do you belittle how real the relationship is between God and his children?" he asked. "I am inviting my friends here to understand that. Do you want to tear down their appreciation of that sacred relationship by reducing it to an exaggeration, a meaningless play on words?"

"We are not talking about them. We are talking about *you*. You sound as if you are claiming to be God's very own son. If that is truly your claim, we say it is a blasphemous claim. If not, then yes, you are playing with words to mislead and deceive."

"You do not misunderstand me," Jesus answered, "but you limit God. You have barely a glimpse of what God is like. Yet you decide his boundaries. You think you know what he can do and what he can't do. So if his son comes in the guise of a prophet, you say 'This does not fit our ideas about God, and so it cannot be.' And if I say I am God's son, then you judge me to be guilty of blasphemy even though I speak the truth."

"There is only one God," their spokesman said. "This is what separates us from the pagans. The God of Abraham is a jealous God who does not tolerate equals or competitors."

"I'm not suggesting that there is more than one God. But I know God as you do not. I don't fault you for that. I'm just saying that you do not fully understand the God you worship."

"Our God has been Lord for a long time—since long before you were born. Our law, our temple, and our traditions have enshrined him in our lives for generations. Do you have any idea how arrogant it is for you first to belittle our practices and now claim to displace our God?!"

"Your God has sent me to call you to true worship. He wants his people to be free. I know you are well-intentioned. But the fact is that you have burdened his children with rules that serve little purpose."

"Our law we have received from Moses."

"Moses led you to freedom. And Moses gave you the Lord's commands. And Moses created rules that were intended to protect order and safety among a people that were unruly nomads. But over the generations your rules and customs have blotted out people's view of the tender love that God has for them."

"Our rules still protect order and safety among our people. Our fear is that people who itch for change will embrace your so-called freedom and abandon their heritage for lawlessness."

"I'm building on that heritage, not destroying it," Jesus said. "I am, in fact, making greater demands than Moses did. Tell me, which is easier: to fast or to forgive an enemy?"

"We have been told that you forgive sins," they pressed on. "Sin is, by definition, an offense against God. And so who can forgive sins but God alone?"

"You know something about sin then," Jesus responded. "But if God gives power to forgive sins to his son, then who is to say that the son can't exercise this power? Your people have found scores of ways to multiply sins and put weights on people's consciences that go far beyond what Moses asked of them. And yet, though you would make them all feel alienated from God for want of petty observances, you would take down a voice that speaks God's mercy and compassion and forgiveness."

A woman in the crowd called to the spokesman from the synagogue. "Sir, I have listened to Jesus many times here. I have seen him cast out devils twice, and I have seen him cure a leper. Doesn't that earn a careful listening? If he tells someone that their sins are forgiven, I certainly would find it easy to believe that they are indeed forgiven."

"Go think about this," Jesus picked up. "Go think about what I say and do. And then ask yourselves, 'Are these the words and deeds of God or of Satan?' If God chooses to send his son to forgive and heal and speak good news, what does that look like? Is God constrained to speak only in thunder and lightning as he did on Mount Sinai? Is God so limited, so confined?

"You are rigid and judgmental in your religious convictions. You turn a loving Adonai into a demanding scorekeeper. And on petty things! I weep for you because your entrenched theology makes it impossible for you to enjoy the loving relationship that the Lord desires with you. But, much worse, you impose that burden on others."

"We have studied the scriptures and the Law," the spokesman said. "We respect them and we do not twist them to our likes and dislikes."

"True, you present yourselves to the people as experts in things that relate to God," Jesus responded. "I have no quarrel with that. Why would I not want God to merit the attention of wise men and scholars? But you think that you know all there is to know about God. You think that the holiness of the subject you study somehow gives you license to lay new burdens on his people and judge their behavior. You want to control people. You are convinced that you are doing them a service in opening for them the gates that lead to God. But they are gates that you have personally erected and controlled! They are gates that close more readily than they open. Do you truly think that God limits the access his children have to him to the one path that you yourselves have built? Can't you see the self-serving pompousness in what you are doing?"

"It is God's burden, not ours, that we broker," the spokesman responded. "We wish you could see that. We wish you would rethink the beauty and importance of the traditions of your own people."

"Let me give *you* a personal invitation," Jesus answered. "My Father has sent me not only to bring his message to these people here but to you as well. Yes, I am angry with your efforts to challenge and dispute my credentials and the authority of my message. But more than that I am sad that you cannot open your minds and hearts to this invitation that God makes to you. If you have ears, listen!"

This last line was not spoken in a scolding tone. It was a plea.

"You are mistaken, sir," the oldest one said. "You are doing religion a disservice. And whether you are willing to recognize it or not, you are putting your own safety at risk." With that they left.

I had been standing in front, next to John. When the discussion finished and the men from the synagogue had left, John shook his head. I looked at Jesus. There were tears in his eyes.

"I get very frustrated with them," he said, nodding in the direction the leaders had gone. "But I'm more disappointed with myself for not finding a way to move them. They are so sincere—and that makes it even more difficult for them to get past the long and deep traditions that they have grown to love. Those who are more passionately committed have a difficult time hearing God's voice in a new way." He too was shaking his head.

I can't remember that I've ever seen him so sad.

✤30✤

Tradition

Think about what I say and do.

I'd recognized two of the religious leaders who attacked Jesus yesterday. They were men for whom I had done work. One is John and the other is Daniel. On an impulse today I decided to talk to them. So I closed the shop early. I'd heard that Jesus wasn't at the lake today anyway. I went to the synagogue and was lucky enough to find them there together.

"We saw you at the lake with him yesterday," Daniel said. "Are you one of his company?" He didn't seem angry, just curious.

"No," I answered. "But I do go regularly to the lake to hear him, and I'm very impressed with him. I'm curious, though. I can understand if you don't want to accept his message. But I am puzzled as to why you seek him out in order to attack him."

"He's dangerous," John answered. "He's luring well-meaning people like you away from the practices that bind us together as God's people. The laws that have been so meticulously developed to help us remain faithful to the law of Moses and the prophets get swept away in his preaching. He practically ridicules them. Don't you see the damage this could do to our faith and our traditions?"

"He only sets them aside to the extent that they are man-made and burdensome." I knew better than to try to win them over. I just wanted to understand their animosity toward this man who to me is so obviously good and just. "He feels that your commands have prevented you from seeing and hearing the heavenly Father who gave us the Law and the prophets in order to help us find him and be accountable to him."

"But don't you see: he has gone too far. People need the discipline to know how to worship God, and he undermines that. Once you begin to pull out a stone here and a stone there, the whole edifice is soon in danger of collapse."

"And he has gotten to the point," Daniel added, "where he thinks he *himself* is God. Perhaps we were too blunt yesterday, and perhaps you are too close to him and too fond of him to see it. But if you try to be objective, you will have to admit that he speaks and acts like he is God's physical son, not just another son of Abraham."

"None of us knows God except for what God has shown us of himself and what is in our hearts," I replied. "I will not pretend to understand it all, but I am willing to believe and accept what Jesus says. With my own eyes, I've seen him restore sight to a blind man. Surely God would not give that kind of support to a liar! He told you yesterday: 'Think about what I say and do.'"

"Life is filled with mysteries," John said. "I don't doubt that you saw what you saw, and I can't explain it. But God having a human son sounds pagan to me and would be even more difficult for me to accept than a so-called miracle."

"Candidly, my friend," Daniel added, "I expect this will all be moot in a short time. I'm sure you don't want to hear this, but there are political implications to his activity. We've heard that powerful men in Jerusalem are very nervous about Jesus. If people begin to perceive him as a messiah and there is risk of their rallying around him as a new King David, the authorities there will do what they must to stop him."

"Do they plan to arrest or kill him?" I attempted to disguise the panic I felt at this news.

"We know of no specific plans," said John, "and we have no firsthand information. But we've heard rumors, and they are easy to believe—we know how those people think."

"And surely you can see," said Daniel, "that Jesus is becoming bolder and more outrageous as time goes by. You might want to think about putting some distance between him and yourself."

"We had hoped that we could do him a favor yesterday by suggesting that he has crossed a line," said John. "But you know; you were there. Clearly he has no intention of turning back."

Nor do I. I have never felt so attuned with my God as I do in my relationship with this Jesus. And as he has said, we must judge people by their fruits.

Jerusalem

❦31❧

Inn at Sychar

*It is not critical whether one worships on
this mountain or that.*

I'm on my way to Jerusalem for the feast, and
I've stopped over in Sychar in Samaria for the
night. I was stunned by the interesting conversation I got into tonight. I didn't really expect
much hospitality since I am clearly from Galilee,
a Jew, and these Samaritans are not known for
their love of Jews. But I told the innkeeper that I
was following a preacher from Capernaum named
Jesus, and he was suddenly very interested.

"That Jesus came through here earlier this week, and my wife is excited about him," he said. "You must talk with her!"

She turned out to be a stately lady, tall and dark and vivacious. She came out to say hello and to ask briefly about my relationship with Jesus. She introduced herself as Leah. She had work to do in the kitchen, but she made me promise that I would not retire until we had a chance to talk. So I nursed my wine and waited, watching the bustle and listening to the conversations around me. There were many Jews at the inn, and, like myself, I supposed, they were headed to Jerusalem for the feast.

As the crowd thinned, the innkeeper's wife finally joined me, accompanied by another lady whom I'd seen waiting tables. Leah introduced her as Rebecca. She was short and plump and, I would guess, five or ten years older than Leah. They sat down with me, obviously anxious to talk about Jesus.

I explained that I have a shoe shop in Capernaum, that Jesus has been preaching in that city, and that I've gone to hear him regularly. "I've been fascinated with his message and, more especially, with the character of the man himself. It's gotten to the point where he recognizes me. He's nicknamed me Soft Shoes! A couple of times I've had the privilege of talking to him alone. Once he read my mind on something we'd not even been discussing. It stunned me!" I hadn't realized how ready I was to share so much information about myself, even with these foreigners. But I think I was filled up with my own experience of Jesus, and it was a relief to talk with somebody about it, especially these women who hung on my every word. Finally I asked them, "So tell me. How do you know Jesus?"

"He came through here early this week," Leah explained. "We have a friend, Sarah, who met him by chance at Jacob's well. They got into an argument somehow. Then he started telling her about her private life. She was so impressed that she made him promise to wait while she got her friends. Rebecca and I and some others went back with her and we were just as overwhelmed by all that he told us."

At this point Rebecca broke in. "There are quite a few of us who think now that he's the messiah. It wasn't just that he knew things about Sarah that no one could possibly know without knowledge from God—it was also the wonderful things he was teaching us."

"We wanted to listen forever," said Leah. "We persuaded him to spend an extra day with us. And we've all heard a remarkable ring of truth in what he says."

Rebecca looked at me carefully and then seemed to decide that it was safe to say more. "We, like you, are looking for the messiah, and this man impresses us as being that person. But we're not sure what to do now. Other than follow his challenge to become better people, we know only to wait."

Leah spoke again. "Don't be offended personally by this, but we've always resented the Jewish arrogance in believing that they have all of the truth. We confronted him with that. Jesus laughed at us. He said, 'In a pagan world of many deities, God chose the Jews as his firstborn. And he loved them in a special way for that. But they have little to brag about. Their whole history is one of defection from loyalty to their Lord and being called back again and again by his prophets.' He told us, 'In this respect, they may be his firstborn but they are a troublesome offspring.'"

"I was raised to be very proud of my Jewish heritage," I said to her. "But I can understand the annoyance that Jesus has, at least with the Jewish leaders. He quarrels with them regularly!"

Leah nodded and continued. "He told us that God's fidelity to the Jews remains almost stubborn. I asked him where that left us Samaritans. He said, 'Abraham and Isaac and Jacob are also your fathers, and more to the point, you are God's progeny, dearly loved by the Lord, whose tenderness and affection are not exhausted by his care for his firstborn.'"

At that moment I began to realize in a most vivid way what it would really mean to follow Jesus. It meant that I would have to look at these women and their families, their community, and welcome them as my own. I'd thought that, in my *mind* at least, I agreed with what Jesus said about God loving us all. But as I spoke with Leah and Rebecca, I could feel myself reacting to them—reacting from deep within, a place I could not reach with my mind. My whole life had created a suspicion in me against these people, and I could not simply wish away those feelings. This is what Jesus meant when he said that our very hearts must change. I was finding it much more difficult to accept the *reality* of Jesus' challenge than I had his words. I didn't say anything but, continuing to listen to the conversation, I was grappling with my deep sense of failing Jesus' mandate to be concerned about all of God's children.

"One of the other women reminded him that we used to have a temple here," Rebecca was saying. "But it was destroyed. Yet the temple in Jerusalem still stands. She asked whether God is sending us a message in that. Jesus explained that God wanted—needed—the Jews to have a temple in their midst. This actually was because of their fickleness. He needed a structure that would remind them every day of his presence in their midst and of their accountability to his laws."

"The temple is a concession to our fickleness?" I countered. "Jesus said that?" The thought took my breath away. "Our temple is more than the center of our worship; it is the center of our identity!"

Rebecca didn't respond to my indignation. "He seemed sad that your temple has become more of a civic gathering spot than a place of prayer and worship. And we asked him, 'But what about *our* temple? Why did God take our temple away from us?' And he said that human pride and fear and hatred lead people to do things that are destructive and have unhappy consequences. It was because of those things that the temple here was destroyed, he said, not because of God's anger toward us. The fact that the temple in Jerusalem stands and ours has fallen doesn't make the Jews better than we are, he said. I remember that he smiled when he said, 'Though they would like to think so.'

"And then he added sadly, 'The day will come—and is not far distant—when that temple too will be destroyed and for the same reasons.'"

"He said that?" I heard from my own startled voice. The women nodded. I was stunned but found my voice. "So did he say whether it is you or we who have the truth?"

It was Leah who responded. "He didn't take sides. He said that goodness is perceived in behavior rather than in creeds and codes. Of course, he said, without the conviction that God holds us accountable to his rules, there is spiritual anarchy. He thinks the Romans are an example of this. He said they have a practice of building their beliefs around their behaviors rather than their behaviors around their beliefs."

"He was careful to note," Rebecca broke in, "that many Romans are just. 'God recognizes them as he did Lot. But,' he said, 'the culture pampers itself and then makes deities out of its vices. No wonder the Lord is a jealous God. How could he not be offended to have his holiness thrown aside for the worship of an invented god who tolerates or even demands debauchery in a place of worship?'"

Rebecca added, "So he told us that even now it is not critical whether one worships on this mountain or that. This is not what distinguishes the children God is pleased with from those who anger him. It is rather the commitment to honesty and concern and generosity that will be the incense taking our prayers to God."

I commented on how like him that sounds. "He is impressive, isn't he?" The apostle of the obvious speaks again! But, in truth, my head was reeling. I was still trying to come to terms with both the enemies-as-friends challenge and the prospect of our temple being destroyed.

Leah said, "We were deeply touched. In fact, we told our friend Sarah that just hearing him talk and listening to what he said is enough to persuade us that this is indeed a message from God and he is God's prophet."

"We wish we could join you in Jerusalem," said Rebecca. "If this is God's messiah, then perhaps this is the feast and the season when he will reveal himself and be recognized. It would be a great privilege to be a part of that."

I replied with irony and without explanation, "We are afraid that this will truly be a memorable feast for him and for us."

We thanked each other and said good night.

❧32❧

Temple

Take your business to the street. This is my father's house.

I've gone to Judea for the Passover celebration. I confess that I'm here less for the Passover than I am to be near Jesus during these days. He has consistently expressed concern for his safety here. Of course, if he's arrested, what help could I be? But I want to be here in any case.

At Bethany on the way in, I stopped to look up his friends Lazarus, Mary, and Martha. They welcomed me as a friend of Jesus. We talked about him, and they invited me to stay with them while I was in the holy city. I told them that I had friends in Jerusalem who were expecting me tonight but asked if I could stay with them tomorrow night. They agreed that I was welcome and said that Jesus also might be staying with them for the Passover.

I went on to the temple and was startled to learn that Jesus had been there earlier and had caused great commotion. A group of the temple moneychangers were just outside the court talking loudly. As I came closer, it was hard to tell if they were angry or simply excited.

It did become clear, though, as I listened to their conversation, that Jesus had tipped over some of the moneychangers' tables and released pigeon doves that were available for sale for the sacrifices. All the while, the men said, he was shouting that they were turning God's house into a bazaar. "Take your business to the street," they quoted him. "This is my father's house!" Apparently this all happened so quickly that the temple security people were not able to intervene.

"We've done business in the temple for years," said one of the men. "And he's crazy if he thinks all of that will change just because today he threw a tantrum!"

I ventured a step or two toward them. "This was Jesus the Galilean?" I asked. They turned to look me over. "I'm a cobbler from Capernaum," I said. "I've heard him preach, and I don't believe he's crazy."

The man who had been speaking glared at me. I felt I should say more. "He is unpredictable. But he has a point. The temple is a place of worship—"

"People come here to make their sacrifices! We make it simple for them. Instead of changing their Roman coins somewhere else and buying their pigeons at another place, they do it all on their way in. We provide a service!"

"We do a legitimate business," one of his colleagues added.

"Do you think Moses or any of the prophets would approve of your doing your business here?" I asked.

"Let the teachers worry about what the prophets would think. This is my work, the way I feed my family, the way I help the people do their religious duties. That crazy Galilean had no business wrecking our tables. That had better be the last we see of him."

"I . . . I've also seen him do miracles," I said, feeling my face grow hot under their gazes. "Look, I'm an educated man, and I've been watching Jesus for some time. I find that usually it's wise to at least consider what he says."

One of the men took a step toward me. "Would you say that you're a friend of his?"

"An acquaintance. We've spoken a few times."

"Then, as his acquaintance, you should tell him that he didn't help himself today, tearing into us like that. We're just businessmen, but we're not the only ones upset with him. This is Jerusalem, after all, and powerful men are behind those walls." He pointed toward the temple. "And they are not happy with this Jesus from Galilee. He'd better watch himself."

"Do these powerful men think he's crazy?" I asked.

"They think he's trouble."

"Does anyone here consider that he might be a prophet?"

The man shrugged. "I don't care who he is. He disrupted my business, as if it was his right to judge me."

They turned their backs on me then, and I didn't say what was on my mind: *None of our great prophets have been popular. People always get angry when a prophet challenges them.* It didn't seem that what I would say could make any difference.

On the way out, I had an interesting conversation with one of the less-agitated pigeon merchants. His name is Quarellus. His thoughts on the incident were interesting. He admitted to losing both money and business because he was one of the targets of Jesus' tantrum. He'd heard stories of Jesus and was glad to have met him, even though he was one of the victims today.

"Actually, the man had a point," he said. "He certainly made me think, and I'll have to decide whether or not to return. Unfortunately, this is a busy and profitable time for us. If I don't offer the service, someone else certainly will, so nothing is accomplished really by going away. But I have to admit that there are some things more important than business. For today I'm seeing my losses as the price for a very thought-provoking lesson."

❦33❧

Third Conversation

My Father has prepared me to cope with the worst in Jerusalem.

I returned to Bethany today, accepting the invitation to stay at the home of Lazarus and his sisters. I had been here only a short time when Jesus arrived with several of his intimates. I offered to move on, but my hosts insisted that they could accommodate everyone for the night. Simon told me about their activities in Jerusalem this day. The highlight was a parade entry into the city with Jesus sitting on someone's donkey while his followers laid out palm fronds and bush weeds as a welcoming carpet for him. I tried to imagine this as they described it, but it was a hard scene to conjure. I wish I'd been there to see it for myself.

After supper, I went out to sit in the night air by myself for a while. I'd been there for some time, trying to sort out things in my head, when Jesus came out and sat with me.

"So you entered Jerusalem with a procession this morning," I began.

He gave a little smile.

"Yesterday the moneychangers and today a triumphal procession! It doesn't look as though you're trying to keep a low profile while you're here."

"I'm just doing what I need to do." The smile was gone now.

"Challenging the moneychangers sounds like you." Here I recounted the substance of my conversation with the moneychangers and Quarellus. "But I can't see you at the head of a *parade.*"

"You may have noticed that I don't control every detail of what happens around me."

"But you sent for the donkey and then rode it into the city."

"And looked ridiculous—to certain people anyway, the ones so worried about my popularity."

I had to think about that. Jesus continued.

"Conquering kings enter a city with majestic horses and legions of soldiers in colorful battle array. They come with trumpets and drums and banners, wearing armor and giving orders. I entered Jerusalem led on a single borrowed donkey, accompanied by a ragtag cluster of peasants who were singing and cheering. It should have been clear to anyone that this 'king' is not a threat to any political power, certainly not to Rome. I doubt they accepted the message, but I wanted to send it to them anyway. At least, if they arrest me, they will be less likely to include my followers in their roundup. It would be a great stretch to read sedition into the joy-filled celebration of that group with me today."

"You still think they will come after you while you're in Jerusalem?"

"I expect so. My Father has prepared me to cope with the worst in Jerusalem."

"Why don't you return to Capernaum? The people there love you. You would be secure among your friends. Then you could continue your preaching."

He was shaking his head before I finished the sentence. "Soft Shoes, I must be here. It's my Father's choice."

After a few silent moments, he stood and wished me good night. He did not reenter the house but instead walked around it to the back area where, I assume, he wanted to be alone to pray.

❧34❧

Paschal Evening

They will certainly kill me.

Our worst fears have materialized. Jesus has been arrested and may even be crucified.

I'd been invited to join the paschal meal with Lazarus, his sisters Mary and Martha, and some other friends at their house. Jesus was having the meal with his intimates at a friend's house in Jerusalem. Our meal was a fine and prayerful event, but the cloud of our fears about the threats to Jesus hung over us the entire evening.

It was long after the meal, and I was the only one still up when James arrived unexpectedly. He was in tears. Several others were awakened by the noise and joined us. James told us that Jesus had been arrested and taken away by a small group of soldiers. He had gone to Gethsemane after the meal to pray and they found him there. James, John, and Simon were the only ones with him at the time.

"How did they find you?" Lazarus asked.

"Our own Jude showed them. After the meal, Jesus had asked everyone to pray, and he told them that he was going to Gethsemane to pray. He asked Simon, John, and me to come with him. So Jude knew where we would be." His face and neck reddened with anger. "After all this time with us—he's nothing but a traitor!"

He looked at us, his face a confusion of rage, fear, and disbelief. "Jude embraced Jesus and then stepped back for the soldiers. I was terrified that we'd all be arrested, but they took only him. I can't believe this," he said, choking on the words.

"We followed," James resumed after he'd gotten himself composed. "We kept at a distance so we wouldn't draw their attention. They took him to the house of the high priest."

"It's absurd that they sent soldiers after Jesus to arrest him," Lazarus said angrily. "So where is he—at Caiaphas's house?"

"As far as I know. Simon stayed there watching. John went to get Jesus' mother. She's in Jerusalem now. I decided to come here. I thought some of you would be here."

Worried and bewildered, we were all silent for a time.

Then, speaking in a soft voice, almost to himself, James began to recount what had happened earlier in the evening.

Jesus had arranged a paschal meal for his intimates and a few other people at the house of a friend in the northwest section of the city. They performed all the usual rituals of the meal. James said that the tone was especially somber. The rubrics of the meal would make it serious in any case but, he insisted, there was a sense of doom that everyone seemed to feel.

"After the second ceremonial cup," James told us, "Jesus began to speak to us. He talked about his need for disciples—people who understood his message and were willing to take on the responsibility of sharing it with others, within Palestine and beyond. He made a special point that this would entail hard work and sacrifice and commitment to prayer.

"He made no secret of the dangers and frustrations that would go with it. 'They will certainly kill me,' he told us, 'and they will do the same to you. The disciples will be treated no better than the master. They will scorn you, reject you, ridicule you, and abuse you in all sorts of ways. They will think that by torturing you and putting you to death they are doing a service to God! But know this,' he said, 'that a new Advocate, the spirit that my father will send, will be with you through all of that. And know also that, though they may pursue and kill you, they cannot extinguish the fire that is this message of good news.'"

Mary said, "It sounds like he expects to die."

James answered, "It does."

"We all heard the warnings," said Mary. "It was as though he'd had a premonition. We just didn't want to listen to that message or believe it. I hope we're mistaken."

James said, "At the dinner, he spoke a long time about God's love for us. It's a theme we heard often in his preaching, but never as tenderly as tonight. He never wavered in his confidence in his Father's love. It was a contagious confidence. I was scared to death, but somehow I felt that I was being held closely in the hands of God. He said that God was requiring his fidelity through this trial. He described it as a redeeming fidelity that would set an example for us and, through us, for many others.

"He promised that he would recruit another witness from among his enemies to help us take his good news to the gentiles. And he told us again about the Advocate who will remind us of what he has taught us."

Now I asked James, "What did he say about Jude—or to Jude?"

"He told Jude that he'd been presented with an enormous choice. We didn't know then what that meant. Jesus spoke to him only briefly. He did say that he loved him. He made that point with each of us.

"Then, when we got to the third ceremonial cup, he broke bread and sent it around. He said, 'This is my body.' And he sent the cup around, saying, 'This is my blood.' He told us that we should repeat that in his memory."

"In his memory?" Lazarus echoed. "He really does expect to die."

"This is my body? This is my blood? He said that?" I asked. "What did he mean?"

"That's what he said. And then he told us to do it in his memory."

As Jews we know the significance of blood. Since our beginnings as a people, we have made blood sacrifices to God—the best of our lambs or cattle. Spilled blood has been part of our covenant with God. We see blood as precious, and we handle it with care. Furthermore, we would never, ever *drink* blood.

Yet Jesus passed around a cup, from which everybody drank, and called it his blood. What was he *doing?*

"When we finished," James concluded, "he led us in a blessing and then we left. I didn't see Jude slip out, but he had gone by then. Jesus asked Simon, John, and me to go with him to Gethsemane to pray. That's where they came for him." James seemed lost in thought then, and his account ended.

I went out to the front of the house and sat down. I can't ever remember being so profoundly sad. I feel guilty. I don't know what I could have done, but I wish I could have done something—anything—to somehow change the course of all that's happened.

I confess that there is fright in my own soul. Will they come after his followers? I keep thinking that people like Simon and James and John may well be taken and executed. If they fear Jesus enough to kill him, then where will they draw the line? I've seen what can happen once soldiers are given an order—they rarely stop at that.

I've often been with Jesus, sometimes even alone. Am I safe? I wonder if that traitor Jude bought his own safety by showing them where they could find Jesus without the crowd.

Tonight we were each overtaken by our own fears—for Jesus and for ourselves. People have heard of Lazarus and what Jesus did when everyone thought he was dead. I'd think that would make Lazarus a target too. Where will this all lead? Where will it end?

I've made time to record my thoughts here. But there are emotions deep in my heart that my pen cannot express.

❦35❧

The Execution

*My God, why have you turned your back
on me?!*

Early today we walked from Bethany to Jerusalem. In the city I saw a lot of his regulars. Is there anyone still in Capernaum today? I also saw most of his intimates. Apparently the officials are not looking for anyone beyond Jesus himself, and everyone is now feeling more free to move about. Word came down at midmorning or so that Pontius Pilate had condemned Jesus to death by crucifixion for inciting sedition. How incredible! It's absurd! The execution took place at

Golgotha. I went there and found a spot at some distance where I could watch. There were three crucifixions; Jesus was the second, in the middle.

I recount all of this with hardly any feeling, or sense. Especially watching from a distance, I could convince myself that it wasn't really happening. There was no self-assured and dynamic Jesus anywhere on the scene. The man I saw was badly beaten, stripped naked, and treated as a criminal. They had pressed into his head a thorn-bush laurel. They nailed him up, just as they have nailed up so many others—spikes driven right through his wrists and feet. I could barely watch when they raised the beam into place. Even from where I stood, I could hear the sounds he made—gasps for breath, grunts of pain. They had nailed a sign to the top of the cross. I couldn't read it from that distance but was told that it said, "Jesus of Nazareth, King of the Jews." I assume that was supposed to be a joke of some kind, the Romans mocking us. I can imagine how those powerful men from the Sanhedrin felt about it.

A few of the other people from Capernaum and a couple of his intimates, Andrew and Levi, stood where I was. We didn't speak, but at first it was comforting to have one another's company. John and some of the women, including his mother, Mary, stood up close. As much as I had wanted to follow him before, I couldn't bring myself any closer to him then. Crucifixion is brutal, but I think it was more than blood that kept me away. I couldn't bear to see my teacher die in such a shameful way. Jesus was dying, but an idea, a dream, was dying too. I understand that now, as I look back on this day. At the time, all I knew was that my legs would not carry me closer to that terrible hilltop.

Toward the end, we could hear him accusing heaven in a voice remarkably strong for a man whose life was ebbing away. "My God, why have you turned your back on me?!" he fairly shouted. That jarred me. I wasn't the only one whose faith had been shaken.

It seemed to take forever for him to die. In the first hour I prayed that his Father would snatch him off the cross, forcing everyone to recognize him as the Lord's own and restoring him to us. I relived the memories of those wonderful days at Capernaum's sea and the times at Zenoff's when he laughed and scolded and taught us. By the end I was just praying that he would die and that his suffering would be over.

Toward midafternoon, the executioners hurried the process along. They broke the legs of the other two men and stabbed Jesus' chest. I'm sure he was already dead by then. When it was over, I saw John lead Mary away. I felt a profound guilt that I was too much the coward to join them. I remembered the day at Zenoff's when John and I had met Mary for the first time. She seems to have feared this end before any of us even considered that it might happen. And I wonder if that makes it any easier to bear. I expect that she is a woman of great faith. But I wonder how even great faith would hold up in the face of this.

I have heard that John will take Mary into his own household—a transaction that Jesus accomplished during his final hours. Already, it seems that this strong yet quiet woman is moving from the outskirts of his ministry to the center of the community he formed. I see, even from a distance, the great respect his intimates have for her. And while it is clear that her grief is excruciating, it is equally clear that her faith in God's care is unwavering.

I returned to Bethany. Several of the others also came to Lazarus's place. No one was hungry. We talked and reminisced a bit. Everything seemed unreal. Some who came later said Jesus had been interred in the tomb of one of his Jerusalem friends, a man named Joseph.

A Joseph brought him up from childhood; a Joseph put his body to rest.

❧36❧

Simon's Lament

God chooses how he will build his kingdom.

It's the Sabbath, and still we are all in a state of shock. The sadness and sense of loss are beyond description. No one wants to think about or talk about those horrible hours when he was on the cross.

Mostly we give voice to our outrage and pain at what has been done to him. Sometimes we babble on about our personal experiences with him. I told about our conversations on the stone fence in Capernaum. Others described how they had come to know him and talked about the impact he'd had on their lives. It seems that everyone in the house had spent time with him individually at least once. There were many touching stories, and we learned about some nicknames that I, at least, had not been aware of. He did have a name for everyone. For as serious as his mission had been, he had a wonderful and clever sense of humor.

Simon had come to join us for a large part of the day. Much of the time he was uncharacteristically silent. Martha had served some supper but we'd just picked at the food. No one had an appetite.

Afterward, I went outside to sit on the stoop where Jesus and I'd had our last conversation just three days ago. It was a warm spring night. The stars were still there. I wondered why God didn't just throw them down on us in anger. Jesus was such a good person and teacher and friend and— what? Prophet? Does that do it justice?

Simon came out then, too. I'm sure he didn't expect to find me there, but I think he was relieved to have someone to talk with.

"What a disappointment we must have been to him," Simon reflected when he'd sat down next to me. "He counted on us and we let him down."

"Don't blame yourself," I said, trying to console both of us. "There is nothing you could have done to stop this. He knew it would happen. He told us it would happen."

"It's not just that he's dead. It's everything. He counted on us, and we let him down."

"What more could you have done? You were faithful disciples. And it was clear to me that he appreciated your friendship and support."

He looked at me for a moment and then at the ground. The silence was heavy but I sensed that I shouldn't break it. Finally he said to me, "You probably didn't hear what happened at the high priest's house?"

I looked at him but didn't say anything.

"There were people coming and going and hanging around," he said. "I kept asking what was happening with Jesus. Most of them didn't know.

A few just said that they were questioning him. Two or three asked whether I was with him."

He paused, and I noticed that he had aged ten years since I saw him last week. His hair seemed grayer. His face muscles sagged. And there was great sadness around his eyes.

"I said to those people, 'No, not at all. I didn't know him personally.'"

I didn't know what to say. All I could do was look at Simon, who stared straight ahead. His speech had dropped to a murmur. "He knew. I told him that I would stand by him no matter what! And he said, 'I know your intentions are noble, Rock. But when the time comes, your fear will get the better of you.'"

"I wasn't there," I said softly. "But I know what it's like when the soldiers are around. The fear can make you do and say things that—"

"It wasn't the soldiers—right then, they weren't around. It was just people coming and going." He put his face in his hands and shook his head.

"Where were the others?" I asked.

"I'm not sure. We got separated in all the confusion."

"James showed up back here. From what I've heard, no one stayed by Jesus."

"I know. My sin is the worst because of what I said. But we've all disappointed him. When I think about the way we've acted—arguing with him when he told us what would happen to him. Trying to keep him from going to Jerusalem. We didn't understand. Or maybe we didn't want to understand."

He slowly looked back at me. "Did you know that James and John had asked for places of honor in his kingdom?"

"When did that happen?"

"One day at the lake. It was during a break and they thought no one else could hear. But I overheard. They asked if they could have the places at his right and left in his kingdom."

"I would think that honor would go to you," I said.

Simon gave a little laugh. "Me too."

"What did Jesus say?"

"He didn't answer the question. He said it was up to his Father. 'God chooses how he will build his kingdom,' he said. But don't you see how we missed his whole message? What a disappointment for him! He preached humility and service—and we are looking for honors!

"His insiders don't get it. His bursar betrays him. His trusted friends want favors. His Rock denies even knowing him. If he expected his work to be carried on by us, he certainly made some bad choices for friends."

What could I say? Will the Advocate he promised find a way to keep his message together in spite of the limitations of its messengers?

"Before the paschal meal, he washed our feet." Simon was looking at me, his eyes revealing some kind of amazement. "Like a servant would do. I was embarrassed."

"But he told us he was sent to serve us, didn't he?"

"He did. But I always thought he meant it in a different way—the way a king serves his people by taking charge."

"I remember, back at the lake, the first time I heard him; he talked about speaking through example," I said.

"After he washed our feet, he told us to love each other the way he's loved us."

After this conversation, Simon decided to leave and return to the upper room where they'd had the paschal meal. Apparently most of Jesus' intimates have gone back there to be together awhile longer. They have so much to talk about and try to make sense of. I've been welcomed to stay here, and I'm going to accept the invitation. I'm too tired to start back. I don't know when or how I'll be able to face Capernaum and its memories.

37

Empty Tomb

I must do what my Father wants of me.

Today we're in an uproar of confusion. We are still reeling from his execution last week. And suddenly there are stories surfacing—about him being alive and that some of the women have seen him. What I know for sure is that the tomb where they put him is empty. The official story from the Romans is that the guards at the tomb fell asleep and his followers stole the body. But his intimates know nothing about it and are as confused as the rest of us.

Of course we would wish him back. I will miss those marvelous days at the lake when he would sit and chat with us or stand and preach in that wonderfully dynamic style to the growing crowds. I will miss seeing his wonders and the faces of those he cured. I will even miss those awkward exorcisms that left all of us feeling exhausted.

How I wish he had not come to Jerusalem. He had been warned. He knew it was dangerous. But then, I know, had he stayed away out of fear, he would not have been Jesus. I recall the day I sat with him on that wall in Capernaum. He'd said, "I must do what my Father wants of me."

Is he really alive? Or is our grief so profound that we are ready to believe in ghosts now? Should we just let him rest in peace—wherever his body is—and try to go on in the spirit of what he preached?

But the man seemed to set aside the laws of nature as easily as he dismissed the rules of our entrenched traditions. And when the women speak of seeing him alive, they are not weepy and hysterical. These are the women who were strong enough to stay close by even while he died in front of them. I have a strange feeling that this story is not over yet.

☙38☙

Inn at Emmaus

*I've assured you that my Advocate will
sustain you through these days.*

This morning I said good-bye to Lazarus
and Martha and Mary and thanked them
for their hospitality. It was helpful to have
the support of their friendship during these horrible days. I set out for home and stopped at the
tavern in Emmaus for lunch.

The place was quite crowded, and there was
a buzz in the air. A man named Cleopas, a resi-
dent of Emmaus apparently, was in the center of a
large group of people. I heard the name Jesus in the

conversation and went over to listen in. I couldn't believe what they were talking about. Yesterday, it seems, this Cleopas and his wife were returning home from Jerusalem and the feast. He was telling how a stranger had joined them and walked with them, and it turned out to be Jesus! Alive!

He was sure of it, he said, because they had many times seen Jesus preach and had, in fact, become followers of his. They hadn't recognized him, Cleopas said, until dinner when, having agreed to stay with them for the night, he broke bread for them. Suddenly it had come together, and they recognized him. And just as quickly as their depression about his death had vanished in joy, he disappeared from their table.

"Where did he go?" one of the men asked him.

"We don't know! He was just suddenly gone!"

"And you went back to Jerusalem?"

"Even in the dark, we risked the trip back. We had to tell the others in his group. And when we found some of them, it turned out that we were not alone. Some of them had also seen him alive."

"I've heard of this Jesus," a stout, gruff man said, "that he works miracles. But don't tell me that someone crucified on Friday is alive today. You were hallucinating."

Cleopas looked at him. "He was as real as your mother-in-law," he said to him with a broad smile. They were obviously friends. And then very seriously, Cleopas went on. "He was as real as any person I've ever met. And it was Jesus for certain. Could my wife and I have imagined the clarity with which he explained how our Scriptures pointed to a messiah who would need to die like the lambs of sacrifice to free us from our sins? I'm not dumb— but I'm not that smart!"

"And the people in Jerusalem have seen him also?" one of the other men asked.

"Several of them. His friend Mary and some of the other women saw him in the morning. And last night, they said, Simon and John and the others were in the room where they had shared Passover with him, and he was suddenly in the room with them. He spoke with them for a while. He told them, 'I've assured you that my Advocate will sustain you through these days.' And then he was gone. It was like our experience. He just vanished."

The conversation continued, but I returned to my lunch, hardly tasting it. By some instinct, my feet moved me back to the road and toward home. It was as if I had to keep moving so that my mind could work with all of this new information.

I had planned to go to bed early. But how can I sleep while the world is changing all around me? All I can do is try to put some of this into words.

There was a time, not long ago, when Jesus represented certain portions of my week—when I would walk down to the lake or over to Zenoff's to hear this man preach and teach. Those days seem far away now, and yet Jesus seems to be everywhere. He has taken over my life!

So. His Papa did not turn his back on Jesus after all.

Jesus lives—he *lives!* What does that really mean? Certainly the whole world must shift. How will our lives change? What will we do now—how will we act—because of this strange and marvelous event?

What new life have we all begun?

Postscript

Today, our scholarship in history, literature, anthropology, and archaeology makes it possible for us to better understand the process that brought us our holy Scriptures. For instance, we know that the Sermon on the Mount was not likely a single sermon delivered on one occasion, as it appears in Matthew or Luke (where it's called the Sermon on the Plain). Rather, the evangelists used their storytelling gifts to put together the counsel of Jesus on a number of topics and in a format that was easy to hear, remember, and retell. Their intention was not to create a court record but to add a written dimension to the story of Jesus as it was being passed on. They were presenting portraits to help people understand the meaning of who he really was.

I have two graduate degrees: one in theology (MDiv) and one in education (MA). For sixteen years, I was a superintendent of Catholic schools, first in the Diocese of Rochester and then in the Diocese of Columbus. But my theology and Scripture studies occurred during an era when Pope Pius XII's encyclical *Divino Afflante Spiritu* had just opened the door to "form criticism" for Catholic biblical scholars. Unfortunately, my seminary professors had chosen not to pass through that door. So my training in Scripture failed to capture much of the excitement that contemporary scholars have teased from the Gospel texts in the last few decades.

Instead, there was a fixation on the literal meaning of the words, and there was much handwringing when passages of Scripture appeared to go in different directions. I remember our Scripture professor arriving in class one day jubilant with a discovery he'd made. "I've reconciled how the sermon was on the mount for Matthew and on a plain for Luke." He stood, leaning over the desk, the tips of his bony fingers supporting him and, with a triumphant grin, announced his discovery. "Jesus went up the mountain—to a plain!" I remember his beaming at us, perhaps awaiting the applause.

Surely, I thought, there is more to the life of Jesus than getting the geographical locations right.

Over the years, my reading and reflection have taken me through the doors where my seminary professors balked. I feel I know the Christ of theology and faith better now than I did as a young man. But the Jesus of history has continued to elude me. The personality of the man who taught by Capernaum's sea and who was arrested and executed in Jerusalem continues to be something of a mystery to me. I'd read the classic accounts of the life of Jesus written a half century ago by Fillion and Ricciotti. But the personality of Jesus didn't really emerge from those pages. I felt sometimes that I knew Thomas Jefferson or Pope John XXIII better than I knew Jesus.

In the last quarter of a century there has been an interest on the part of Scripture scholars to find the "historical Jesus." Their studies and analyses have been interesting and helpful but are, in the end, frustrating. Depending on the historical methods accepted, the "historical" data about Jesus are skimpy indeed. Jesus lived, taught, and was executed. The Jewish historian Josephus tells us that much. Details beyond that are filtered through the memories and faith of his early followers. The color that emerges through that prism is impossible to trace back to tell whether its origin is the Jesus of history or of faith. Historical analysis wrestles with whether he might actually have said this or done that. But in the end it still is able to say little about him as a personality.

Of course *The Shoemaker's Gospel* is not a historical biography. It fits into the category of historical fiction, a novel that puts events, characters, and words around a well-known personality and, perhaps, captures in the process the man at the core of it all. In the end I hope that I have not created a fictional Jesus. I hope rather that, in stories and dialogue, I have fleshed out somewhat the Jesus I have known since I was introduced to him as a child many decades ago. The exercise has been helpful to me. Like the shoemaker, I write to crystallize my thinking about life and God and politics and relationships. The reflections that produced the journal entries of the shoemaker helped me to rediscover Jesus, as I believe each Christian must do from time to time. I hope the reader also has found here his or her Jesus. I hope you too have been able put yourself into the character of the shoemaker and found a fresh perspective on our Teacher and Friend.

Because it is the person of Jesus whom God sent to us as his revelation about himself—and us.

Acknowledgments

I'm very indebted to Bill Shannon and Lisa Biedenbach, whose belief in this project kept it alive.

And I want to give special thanks to the wonderful people at Loyola Press. Joe Durepos's enthusiasm championed the book and he served as cheerleader throughout the process. Vinita Hampton Wright, a gifted storyteller herself, edited the manuscript and stretched my abilities. And I'm grateful to Rebecca Johnson, Leslie Waters, Yvonne Micheletti, and all the others behind the scenes who did the heavy lifting to produce the volume.

I especially appreciate the "Rooster Group," whose encouragement has been so helpful in this project. I am also indebted to Father Ray Booth and Sam Lacara, whose suggestions made this a better book. And I owe thanks to Larry Lancto, whose proofreading of the original manuscript rescued me from the embarrassment of typos and misplaced commas! Rest in peace, Larry.

And I thank the Lord, who wrote the plotline and whose life and teaching have challenged me over all these years.

Dan Brent

LOYOLA & CLASSICS

Catholics	Brian Moore	0-8294-2333-8	$11.95
Cosmas of the Love of God	Pierre de Calan	0-8294-2395-8	$12.95
Dear James	Jon Hassler	0-8294-2430-X	$13.95
The Devil's Advocate	Morris L. West	0-8294-2156-4	$12.95
Do Black Patent Leather Shoes Really Reflect Up?	John R. Powers	0-8294-2143-2	$12.95
The Edge of Sadness	Edwin O'Connor	0-8294-2123-8	$13.95
Helena	Evelyn Waugh	0-8294-2122-X	$12.95
In This House of Brede	Rumer Godden	0-8294-2128-9	$13.95
The Keys of the Kingdom	A. J. Cronin	0-8294-2334-6	$13.95
The Last Catholic in America	John R. Powers	0-8294-2130-0	$12.95
Mr. Blue	Myles Connolly	0-8294-2131-9	$11.95
North of Hope	Jon Hassler	0-8294-2357-5	$13.95
Saint Francis	Nikos Kazantzakis	0-8294-2129-7	$13.95
The Silver Chalice	Thomas Costain	0-8294-2350-8	$13.95
Things as They Are	Paul Horgan	0-8294-2332-X	$12.95
The Unoriginal Sinner and the Ice-Cream God	John R. Powers	0-8294-2429-6	$12.95
Vipers' Tangle	François Mauriac	0-8294-2211-0	$12.95

Available at your local bookstore, or visit **www.loyolabooks.org**
or call **800.621.1008** to order.

Join In. Speak Up. Help Out!

Would you like to help Loyola Press improve our publications? Become one of our special Loyola Press Advisors. From time to time, registered advisors will be invited to participate in brief online surveys. We will recognize your efforts with various gift certificates, points, and prizes. For more information, visit **www.SpiritedTalk.org**